Jack Smith

Tucker Amory's 2nd Senior Year

Jack Smith

Sharon, Pennsylvania

Shenango River Books
P.O. Box 631
Sharon, Pennsylvania 16146

First Edition, Summer, 1996.

Cover art and design by Mike Reznor.

Printed in the United States of America.

ISBN 1-888836-03-2

For Pat,
Robin and Bob, Claudia and Orby,
Mary and Jack, Germaine and Chris,
Nell and Jesse

Tucker Amory's 2nd Senior Year

One

In case you want to know, I flunked all my subjects my senior year in high school, even gym if you can believe that. I probably would've flunked study hall, but they don't give a grade for it. Some kids who flunked dropped out of school and went to work in the stinkin' mills. I didn't do that, though, and I can't really say why.

In the middle of my second senior year, I got kicked out of English class because I refused to do a dumb homework assignment, got kicked out of homeroom because Old Gussie thought I'd spent too much time in a boys restroom, and finally got suspended from school, for jumping the assistant principal and trying to beat him up. After all that you'd think I'd have ended up in reform school, or something. It was some kind of miracle I didn't. That's what this story's all about.

When I went to bed the night before the first day of the new school year, I'd hoped for rain. A raincoat and maybe even an umbrella would have given me cover, since I felt like a criminal, anyway. But the sun was out, bright and warm. A morning when you'd rather be riding your bike or sitting on a sandy beach with your girl and working on a tan.

I waited in the house, until I was sure the street was clear of kids on their way to school. It was a long wait, Wendell S. Cruhl High School being only half a block from Grandmom's house, and a lot of kids coming this way.

I had planned my moves very carefully. When I was sure the way was clear, I sneaked through the front door, stepped quietly off the front porch, made a quick left turn at the end of the walk, and strolled nonchalantly up the street to school.

"Hi, Tucker," she said, smiling. She started to say more but stopped cold. I guess she remembered and felt sorry for me.

Ingrid was a classmate and an honor student. She was not very attractive, kind of heavy and square-built, you might say. She wore German pigtails and had really thick lips. Her family came from Germany in 1937 to escape the holocaust. Her father's an electrical engineer, brilliant, and very eccentric. He'd walk all the way home from his job at Westinghouse talking to himself. Most kids in the neighborhood were in awe of Ingrid's family.

Ingrid's always been very kind. Once when I was a little kid and scraped my knee pretty bad and had to wear a bandage that made me limp, I told her I'd broken my leg, just to make an impression. She pretended to believe me.

Ingrid wasn't going to school this morning: she graduated last spring. I should have too, as I said before. So there I was, on the day after Labor Day that fall, 1949, the first day of a new school year. Kind of weakly, trying to hide my shame, I said hello but didn't stop to talk.

It wasn't because I was dumb that I flunked my senior year. Though in some classes I felt pretty dumb. In math, for instance, I'd learn the rules and do the problems, and usually I'd get correct answers, but when I closed the book and later sat for a test, by then I'd forgotten everything. Like someone had opened my head and took everything out. I just couldn't retain anything about math.

In other subjects, like history or English, boredom stymied me. I'd sit at the kitchen table at night with books open, and just stare at the pages. Soon I got so far behind the whole idea of doing homework overwhelmed me, and I just gave up. That's the way it had been, ever since first grade. But I always managed to get by, somehow. Just barely. In public school if you're dumb or exasperate the teachers in some way they sort of give up after a while and pass you anyway. I guess that lulled me into believing I'd never be held back. Even as the F's piled up around me, I felt I'd graduate with my class.

To tell the truth, though, my flirting with failure goes all the way back. I actually did flunk first grade.

I was five, and my mom took me to a school to enroll me. I remember visiting a classroom and meeting a teacher who seemed real nice—young and pretty like my mom. The kids' desks had wooden tops and seemed very old. They had ink wells and were scratched and stained, but not so bad you couldn't write on them. They stood on fancy black iron legs and were bolted to the floor, a wooden floor that squeaked a little. Slate blackboards covered all but one wall which was all windows. Posters and crayon drawings looking like they'd been done by first graders covered the walls in some places. And someone had written the alphabet neatly in longhand across the top of the chalkboard behind the teacher's desk. There was just something about it all that made me eager to start school.

But when the teacher found out I wouldn't be six until January, she told my mom I'd have to wait a year. I was really disappointed. When I did start school the following September, a lot had happened by then. My mom had heart trouble and had to spend a lot of time in bed, my dad started drinking and didn't come home nights, and by then I'd changed: I'd become a little unmanageable. The housekeeper my dad hired to do what mom couldn't didn't know how to control my misbehavior, like the time I crawled under Mom's bed while she was sleeping, and the housekeeper couldn't find me anywhere and called the cops.

My first grade teacher was old and cranky. She wouldn't let us kids forget she was retiring at the end of the school year, because, she said, we were a bunch of ne'r-do-wells. I sat in the back of the room and tried to shut out her complaints about us. When things really got bad, I took out my frustration on my notebook. It had one of those black and white marbled covers you see even today. I'd dig deep holes in the pages with the point of my pencil or draw angry swirls. I remember that, every time I see notebooks like mine.

What a year! My teacher being hateful, my dad drinking and staying out late, my mom ill and bedfast, and then I got sick! An ear infection that was so bad a specialist had to be called in. He gave me sulfa drugs, I had an allergic reaction, and it ended up I was out of school seven weeks. That and my bad behavior in and out of school made me flunk first grade. But as things turned out I didn't have to repeat. We moved! Mom and I went to live with Grandmom back in Coaltown, Pennsylvania. It was because it was the Depression and Dad lost his job and he and Mom separated.

When September came, Mom dressed us up in Sunday clothes and off we went, to see the principal of the neighborhood school. Miss Quack was her name, honest to god. Mom conned her with my sad tale—all that had happened to cause me to flunk, and I got put in second grade.

As it turned out, I liked my second grade teacher. Miss Mylot was her name. She was patient and kind and made learning fun. I did my work in school, homework too, and passed. I didn't have real trouble again until high school, which brings me back to where I started.

After leaving Ingrid standing on her porch, I walked to the corner, waited for the light to change, and crossed over.

Wendell S. Cruhl High School is a big, red brick blob of a building. It's not worth describing. Faceless, like a lot of schools everywhere. The lobby though is a surprise. Real white marble everywhere, honest to god. The floor, the steps, the walls, even the ceiling. Everything glistens in cold, milky whiteness. You'd think it was a museum. There are two life-size white marble statues of historical figures wearing colonial costumes. They guard the steps leading up to the doors leading into the main corridor. In the center of the steps is a shiny brass handrail. The janitors have orders to polish it daily. Anyone who is seen touching it runs the risk of being stopped by the assistant principal, Mr. Feralman. There's a rumor he has everyone's finger prints on file. No student is permitted to use the main entrance. Once when I was suspended from school for three days and couldn't get back in unless my parents came with me, I made a point of using the main entrance. When we reached the steps, I deliberately laid my greasy fingers all over the shiny brass rail and smeared my prints, just in case Feralman really did have them on file in his office.

On this, my first day of my second senior year, I entered through a side door, and, just as I turned a corner on my way to the auditorium, bumped shoulders with Jimmy Hartung, a guy in the class I should have graduated with. "Hey, Amory, watch where the hell yer goin!" Ignoring him, I trotted ahead, avoiding anything he might say to embarrass me. I wondered for a moment why he was in the building.

From the hall I could hear the principal, Mr. Blott, talking to the student body assembled in the auditorium. He was preaching as usual—all about trying one's best and how the teachers were there to help them and if anyone had a problem his door was always open, which was a lot of bull because he was never there, door open or not!

I tiptoed in, so as not to attract attention, and took a seat in the last row. I know it was really dumb to try to make myself invisible. Soon everyone who didn't know I failed would know, and I'd have to face up to it. Blott finished his sermon with a few threadbare words: "If at first you don't succeed, try, try again." Everybody groaned and rose to go to classes. I hurried out ahead and dragged myself to my first period class.

I don't remember very much about that first day. I didn't make eye contact with anybody. Being as I was dumb, I was given the easiest subjects a senior could take. They gave me Consumer Math, Problems of Society, and Sales and Merchandising, and, of course, remedial English. I suppose they'd have given me Home Ec, if guys were allowed. It felt funny seeing younger kids taking over the leadership of clubs and such. I didn't belong to any, and everyone pretty much let me alone.

September went by, and I closed my mind to everything. Funny thing was, I dressed up for school. I shined my shoes, wore carefully pressed dress trousers, a dress shirt and necktie, and sometimes a sport coat. I caught a lot of jeers from the guys, especially the athletes, but I didn't care. I guess my clothes were kind of a shield that kept everyone at a distance.

"Hey, Amory, where da ya think ya are, Sunday School?"

"Where's the funeral, Amory?"

"If yer gonna flunk, do it in style, right, Amory?"

As the days passed, I noticed things were changing. Friday night dances after football games had always been popular. Now it seemed no one went. I sat by myself, listened to the juke box, but danced with no one, and left early.

After school there didn't seem to be anywhere to hang out anymore. Walter's Lunch Counter, Rogan's Dairy, the Sunoco Station owned by Ray Hanky's dad—all were empty. All the guys I'd hung around with had enrolled in college or taken jobs in the mills. Most of the time I walked the streets alone. Once in a while I'd run into somebody from one of my classes and b.s. for a while. Other times I stayed home, daydreamed, or listened to the radio. The programs were mostly boring stuff like *Just Plain Bill, Jolly Rhythm Boys, Portia Faces Life, When a Girl Marries.* Mostly silly soap operas.

Weekends were really depressing. I filled my time going to movies. On Saturday and Sunday, I was the first one in the door for matinees, and I stayed until the last showing, around midnight. I sat in a front row seat, with my feet propped up on the railing, practically nose to nose with the screen. Looking up all day sometimes gave me a pretty stiff neck.

If I got bored, I moved on to a different theater. There was the Columbia, a big, elegant theater. It had live shows, along with movies because there was a stage. The Liberty, the Nuluna, and the Gable were smaller. The Gable was a rundown rat trap that catered mostly to kids and showed cowboy, gangster and adventures. It stood beside railroad tracks, and when a train went by it shook the screen and drowned out the sound. One weekend I saw every movie in all four theaters. I saw Monte Hale in *Law of the Golden West,* Abbot and Costello in *Buck Privates Come Home,* Wild Bill Elliott in *The Last Bandit,* Adele Jurgen in *Ladies of the Chorus,* Bing Crosby and Bob Hope in *Road To Rio,* Humphrey Bogart in *Knock on Any Door*, Robert Mitchum in The *Big Steele,* James Cagney in *White Heat,* and Ron Randall in *The Lone Wolf and His Lady.* I guess you could say I saw a lot of movies. It took hours sometimes just to get my eyes to focus on anything farther away than ten feet.

Mom said my marathon movie-going weekends were unhealthy. She urged me to get an after-school job delivering papers or maybe ushering in one of the theaters. But there never seemed to be any openings, and besides I didn't know how to apply for a job. But Mom found a job for me. The owner of the photo studio that did senior pictures and yearbook snaps offered me a job as door-to-door salesman of family portraits.

"You show the customer the samples in this kit," Mr. Amos said. He was a bald, skinny little guy. He opened a leatherette salesman's case that had pockets containing color-tinted portraits in different sizes, order forms, and a price list. There was even a cheap ball point pen tucked into a loop.

"Your father would be proud, Tucker," Mom said, as if I cared what he thought.

"You set your own working hours," Mr. Amos added proudly, expecting me to be impressed. "The more hours you work the more you earn, ten percent commission on every order you sell."

I didn't want this job, but I couldn't think of a way to worm out of it. For a few days I went from door to door in my neighborhood. Lack of confidence in myself made me very self-conscious. Mr. Amos told me what to say.

"Good afternoon. My name is Tucker Amory. I represent Michelangelo Studio of Photography. May I have a few moments of your time? I'd like to tell you about a special on family portraits."

A few neighbors did take an order from me for studio appointments, but some were annoyed at being disturbed in their homes, and some didn't answer the door. So I quit.

One evening late in September when I was alone in the house and there was nothing on radio worth listening to, I found a book of short stories among Mom's stuff. The first story it opened to was "Paul's Case" by Willa Cather, a story about a guy my age who lived in Pittsburgh with his family he couldn't stand. Pittsburgh's a smoky city right near Coaltown. Honest to god, sometimes you have to turn on your headlights in broad daylight just to keep from crashing into other cars, there's so much smoke. Well, I have to tell you about this story because it really shook me up.

Paul's this guy's name. He doesn't get along with his parents, he's flunking out of school, he dresses up in fancy clothes, and he spends all his time in theaters. Just like me! By the time I got to the end, I was shaking all over. The only thing different was, the story happened about the year 1900. You have to know that because of his clothes. He wears velvet collars and a stick pin in his necktie.

Paul's called into the principal's office because he's been insolent. But he's not punished. It seems the principal is so exasperated with him he doesn't know what to do. Paul leaves the office full of contempt for the principal and all adults he's ever known. He struts off to a concert hall where he works ushering. Paul's an artsy kind of guy: he likes palatial surroundings, dreamy music, and theater people. After the last performance, he trudges home to the all-too-real lower middle class family he belongs to. On this particular night he sleeps in the basement because he can't stand to face his father. He hates his father.

A few days later, the principal goes to see his dad. It's decided that he'll be taken out of school, out of the job he loves, and they all hate, and be put to work full time running errands in some dreary office building. Time goes by and Paul is miserable in this new job. One day Paul's boss sends him to the bank to deposit a large sum of money. This is Paul's big chance. He pockets the money and runs. He takes a train to New York City, buys tailor-made duds, rents a suite of rooms at the Waldorf-Astoria Hotel. At night he dresses white tie, eats at fancy places like El Morocco, and goes to the opera. He hob nobs with a rich kid in the hotel and throws money around. Naturally it can't last, and he knows it. Curious about what's happening back in Pittsburgh, he picks up a copy of the *Post-Gazette* and finds a story about himself and the theft. It says his dad restored the funds and is in New York City hunting for his son. The game is up. So Paul takes out a pistol he bought, but he can't force himself to use it. Instead, he takes a taxi to a railroad station, and would you believe it, throws himself in front of a speeding train! Wham! No more Paul!

Oh, man, did that shake me up! It could have been me. Escaping into fantasies. Dressing up for school. Hating my parents, especially my dad. Being more artsy than athletic. I don't think I could have stolen a lot of money and run away. I wouldn't have had the guts to do that. But in everything else, I felt like a carbon copy of poor old Paul. The suicide part was too frightening to think about.

Maybe you think reading that story changed me somewhat. It only made me more anxious. It takes more than reading a story to make a guy change, like with failing senior year. Nothing I see or hear or do badly ever makes me act any different.

Two

"What the heck happened to you?"

"I don't want to talk about it," he said.

Jerry Small was a kid in my gym class. Like me he wasn't very big, and he was kind of sensitive and quiet. He came to school one day in October with his face bruised, like he had an accident or been in a fight. Other kids too had been coming to school lately looking like they'd been in a fight and wouldn't tell what happened.

Cruhl High School in those days could sometimes be a crazy place. Like when I returned from Chicago during the summer of my freshman year, and I heard some of the violent things that went on. There was a tradition, for instance, that the junior and senior guys have a class fight every October in the streets of Coaltown. This had been going on several years. No one seemed to know how the tradition got started. When school opened in September, there would be a lot of talk and anticipation. The cops tried to discourage it. They didn't exactly drool over the prospect of having to try to stop a street fight involving about a hundred guys. The class officers kept mum about the exact date, so the cops couldn't stop it before it got started. All during late September and early October the nights were electric with anxiety. I didn't give it much thought during my underclassman years. But there was plenty of tension around school and lots of warnings about staying off the streets at night. When it did happen, I didn't know until the next day, when guys would come to school all battered and bruised and school officials would call an assembly and give everybody hell who took part. When I became an upperclassman the tradition stopped for some reason, and the class officers were pretty tight-lipped about it. It couldn't have been pressure from the cops; they could never stop anything guys were determined to do. Recent grads were shocked when they heard, and called us all a bunch of pantywaists. Even some of the dads! I actually heard one dad say his son's friends were all a bunch of cowards. Really! I'm not kidding, he'd actually been looking forward to the big brawl.

One day about this time, a warm day when lots of fallen leaves were still on the ground, I was on my bike, pedaling to the drug store to pick up a prescription for Grandmom's arthritis. This guy I hardly knew came up behind me and grabbed the back of my bike, forcing me to stop. Two of his buddies joined him, all three of them big guys who liked to taunt littler kids.

"Hey, Amory, where ya goin', kid?"

I didn't say where, because I knew they'd jump on that, so I just said I was riding around for the hell of it.

These guys belonged to a gang that lived in the flats, a seedy part of downtown. Tight-fitting tee shirts. Pack of smokes folded into a sleeve. Arrogant as hell. I was just a puny kid, too small to put up a defense, which made me an especially sweet target.

The one who stopped me stuck out his chin like Mussolini and sneered, "You never lived in Chicago, shit-ass! That's just a dumb lie you tell to impress the titless broads you date."

One of the flunkies chimed in with, "You know what Tucker, eh! eh!, rhymes with, right men? eh! eh!?"

"I went to junior high in Chicago," I said, as calmly as I could, so as not to give them anything to pick up on. "It was a long time ago. I don't know why you'd be interested."

The third goon, a real cretin who spoke like he had a mouth full of marbles, mocked my words, "Bug thuty kud, huh!" And that's all he said.

The leader had thick arms that swung heavily from his shoulders like lead weights. I found out later his name was Spondike. "What ya know about the Bears? See any games at Soldier Field?"

"I saw the Bears play the College All-Stars, the year Tommy Harmon quarterbacked." This brought real surprise to their faces. "I lived in an apartment across the street from Wrigley Field. I watched home games from my fifth floor living room window. The stadium wall was low at that point in left field, and you could see over it. One day I saw Joe Dimaggio hit a homer against the Cubs."

All of this was a lie, but they really soaked it up. Next they wanted to hear about city life. I told them how I rode the subway, called the I.C., into the Loop. "A train ran over a kid's foot once. Chopped off all his toes. Left him with a stump wrapped in a bandage. After that we nicknamed him Q-Tip." I was really on a roll, and they hung on every word. "I saw great things in museums. There's the Museum of Science and Industry. They display dead fetuses in jars of formaldehyde, each at a different point of gestation, from a mere embryo to a baby ready to pop out of a mother's uterus." I said I didn't know what had killed the fetuses. When I'm nervous like I was, I ramble on and hardly know what I'm saying. But it worked. They stood frozen in their tracks, wide-eyed and open-mouthed. Just long enough for me to goose the pedals of my bike and take off.

Later it occurred to me that the Cubs were not in the same league as Dimaggio. If I hadn't snowed them with my tall story, they'd have killed me.

When I finally got home with Grandmom's prescription, I was an hour late and caught heck from Mom. But I didn't tell what happened; I was too embarrassed.

Growing up I was always the kind of kid bullies picked on. At the start of my second senior year, I was eighteen, five foot eight, and weighed about a hundred and forty pounds. Girls said I was good-looking, but the best-looking girls went for athletic types or guys with great personalities. Me? I was shy. I was okay, except in a crowd. For some reason I sat back and let others be the life of the party. It's funny, because I liked parties and being with lots of people.

The number of guys coming to school with bruised faces and refusing to talk about it grew steadily. The assistant principal, Mr. Feralman, called the beat up guys into his office one day, demanding to know what was happening. The injured were not members of any particular clique, though they did seem to be the brainy guys and the ass-kissers. All kept their mouths shut. Feralman thought he saw a pattern in it, so he called an assembly of all boys in Cruhl School, as some of us called it. Feralman ranted and raved, but no one squealed.

While all this was going on, I opened my locker one day to put my books away, and out fell a little white card with the words "YOUR NEXT!" printed on it. It was a business calling card. I had to chuckle at the spelling. Spelling!

One thing I was always good at. I didn't pay much attention to it, the card that is. I stuck it in my pocket, wondering what I was going to get. I found out, though, pretty quick.

It happened on a Tuesday night, at a midweek dance at the Josephenium, which was a gym at St. Joe's, the Catholic Church.

Everyone went stag and dressed real casual. Guys sat on one side of the floor, girls on the other. A Wurlitzer belted out popular love ballads and jitterbug jazz tunes. I was sitting on a bench b.s.ing with the guys and eyeing the girls, when this guy came up to me. "You got the card, right?" Stiff, greasy duck-tail, cheap white tee shirt, trouser cuffs rolled calf high, revealing white socks and a pair of black steel-toed mill-worker shoes.

"What card?" I asked, innocently.

"You know damn well what card, Amory, the one I put in your locker this morning!"

"Oh, yeah, that one," I said, playing dumb.

"What is it with you, Amory, you chicken?"

I didn't answer, nor did I move off the bench.

"You're a god-damned little coward, Amory! Are you gonna come outside and fight like a man? Or are you gonna sit there all night and show all the handsome boys and pretty girls what a stinking coward you are?"

"Fight about what?" I stammered.

This was embarrassing—him crouched down, dodging and weaving, and me frozen in terror, my sweaty palms gripping my knees, while Perry Como crooned "How Do I Love You" on the Wurlitzer, and couples danced cheek to cheek around us. Failing to talk me off the bench, he began to tremble with rage, his face a ripe tomato. I'd had my share of street fights growing up, but nothing like this kid before.

"I don't know you! I've no reason to fight!"

This enraged him even more. He cocked his arm to throw a punch, but his goons stopped him. "Not here," one said, and pulled him away.

Then I recognized him—Spondike, the bully who stopped me on my bike. "What's a matter, Tucker, too chicken to fight?"

"Go on, he can't hurt a fly!" This came from a guy waltzing by and trying to impress his partner.

"I could hear sneers and snickers all around me, and my face got hot. I had mixed feelings. I felt relieved but ashamed. Something told me I should have gone outside with Spondike, while another voice said no: there had been no reason to fight and saying so had defeated him in a way no fight could. But damn it! In a situation like this there is no right way. I guess you just have to do what your instinct says. I looked at my watch and saw it was almost time for the dance to end. So I left.

Outside, I hurried along the street, twisting past people, when suddenly I heard heavy footsteps behind me. My heart jumped, but I didn't turn around.

"Hey, Tucker, wait up." It was Michael Mink, a guy in math class.

"Jesus, you scared me. Did you see what happened back there?"

"Yeah, I saw. You got one of these too, uh?"

He showed me a card like the one that bastard put in my locker. "I guess I must be next on his list," Michael said, trembling.

We walked along together. "What should I do, Tucker? What could Bill Spondike have against me? I hardly know him.!"

"You saw what I did, do the same. Why should any guy have to be suckered into being Spondike's punching bag? He's a body builder, for Christ's sake. They say he works out every day at Muscle Mania!"

"I don't know. Everyone's thinking you're yellow. I can do without that tag being stuck on me."

"All the more reason to say no. So who's the real coward, anyway? I'd like to see what'd happen if he went up against someone in his own league, which I bet he doesn't do."

"I don't think I have much choice, Tucker." And with those words, he trotted off.

When I got home, I unfolded my bed, a roll-away I slept on in Grandmom's dining room because I didn't have a room of my own. I buried my face in my pillow and wept.

The next day in Spigelmeyer's study hall, I was handed a note saying that Mr. Feralman wanted to see me in his office. I had a pretty good idea what it was about, being as I hadn't been in any trouble lately in school.

"I hear you had a little adventure last night," Feralman said, sarcastically.

Mike Mink and his parents were there. Feralman leaned across his desk, and cat-like stared me down, purring. "I've heard Mike's version. Now I want to hear yours. Boys coming to school everyday with battered faces!"

He tried to make it sound like he really cared, when all that really mattered to him was solving an ongoing problem that had begun to make him, school disciplinarian, look weak.

So I told him what happened between me and that goon Spondike, at the Josephenium. I didn't like having to say I refused to fight. Feralman had a look in his eye that made me feel like a coward, but he pretended that I had done the right thing, and defended Michael's coming to him about it all, which was Michael's way of squirming out of having to fight Spondike at some future time, because now the cat was out of the bag and Spondike would be stopped. At least that's how it looked to me.

"I admire Michael's coming to me. That was brave. Spondike threatened him with a beating should he come to me. Isn't that right Michael?"

This was just grandstanding for the benefit of Michael's parents. They, of course, smiled proudly at Michael, you know, the way parents do when they praise something that doesn't deserve it.

"Dr. Hammond will be notified, and a disciplinary hearing will be held, now that I've rooted out the truth," Feralman crooned, his thumbs hooked serenely into the pockets of his vest.

By the way, Dr. Hammond was superintendent of schools. We called him Dr. Spam because he looked kind of greasy and left a bad taste in our mouths.

Mr. Feralman gave Mike and me passes so we'd be admitted to our class. About a week later we were called to a meeting of the school directors.

Spam was in charge. His doctorate, by the way, was honorary, awarded to him by his alma mater, for no reason that anyone in Coaltown seemed to know, except maybe that Spam's cousin was a trustee of the college. Spam dressed better than most male teachers, in tailor-made suits. Most men looked all alike because they all bought theirs in Coaltown's only department store that sold only one cheap brand.

Besides Spam, Feralman, and the school directors, there were Spondike, his goons, all the guys who'd been beat up, and their parents. There was no doubt about who was guilty and who was innocent. Spondike had nothing to say for himself, nor did any of the victims. But the parents and school directors had plenty of words for the culprits.

"Considering the weight-training you've had, you had an unfair advantage over your victims, and you knew it!" accused Dr. Hammond. Spondike's eyes gave off an evil glow through it all. If Spam thought Spondike could be shamed, he was wrong.

The hearing lasted an hour. It ended with a decision to suspend the boys for ten days and to revoke all their social privileges for the remainder of the school year. Parents were angry. They demanded expulsion. I was disappointed because Spondike was not asked for an explanation of his behavior, nor an apology. And, I thought Spondike was a little crazy, but no one said anything about counseling, and I sure as hell didn't mention what was not in my place to say anything about. So that ended it.

Three

The crap Spondike stirred up had me feeling pretty bad about myself, but one day something happened to make me forget about it for a while. It was a day early in November, and Señorita Witherspoon, the Spanish teacher, called me into her classroom, though I was not one of her students, and asked me to close the door.

"My, my, Tucker, how nice you look!" She eyed me up and down. She was very pretty. "I called you in here because I have a favor to ask of you. The Armistice Day Assembly will be held soon, and I would like you to recite a little prepared speech."

She spoke very slowly and deliberately, chewing every word like it was a tasty piece of meat. At first I thought it was because she thought I was retarded that she spoke this way, but I learned later she spoke like this to everyone; she was from the deep South and had an accent. But there was a rumor she wasn't a southerner, that she grew up in Yankee Lake, a farm town on the other side of the county, and that she had gone south to study Spanish. Then came back to Pennsylvania speaking like Scarlett O'Hara, the name her students tagged her.

"No, you don't want me for this job!"

"Why not, Tucker, honey? You are such a prepossessing young man. You dress so smartly for school every day, and you have such self-assurance!"

Is this really me she's talking to? I thought. It was always a smart kid or teacher's pet that got picked. How could she not know I was a flunky?

"It's true, I don't know you very well, but something in your demeanor tells me—" Before she finished the sentence, her eyes dimmed a little and her voice dropped, "—you're just the boy I want."

A little tingle went up my spine.

"You are a handsome young man, and I bet you've got lots of stage presence."

No one had ever spoken to me like this—not my girl friends, and not even my mom!

"Thank you for the compliments, Miss O'Hara—I mean Señorita. But I don't think I could handle it. I'd be awfully nervous, and I'd probably forget the words."

Ignoring my little nervous mistake with her name, she said, "No problem there, Tucker. I'd be standing behind the curtain, with a copy of the speech in my hand, and would prompt you, should you forget even one itty-bitty word."

She handed me a single sheet of paper, covered with large type, triple spaced. I could see there wasn't much to memorize. "Take it home, read it over, and give me your answer tomorrow."

I thought I detected perfume on the paper, or maybe it was just her sweet words. She sure had me buffaloed and tongue-tied. I couldn't admit I was just a dumb guy no teacher ever trusted, and that I'd probably forget to show up at the assembly.

During Problems of Society I read it over. It was all about dead soldiers buried in foreign lands, how their sacrifice was remembered on this day, and how the living owed them a debt of gratitude. It made me think of the story Mom had told me about my Uncle Fred, how he had left home for the trenches in France in 1917, and how his dad was dying at home at the time, and the two of them saying good-bye, knowing they'd never see each other again, which was the truth, because his dad, my granddad, died three months later without ever knowing whether his son came home from the war. So I sort of got caught up in it all. I started to think about how I'd say the words at the assembly. I pulled myself up in my seat, knit my brow like a Sunday preacher, and imagined myself standing before the whole student body.

"Tucker Amory!" The angry voice of Third World War, the teacher, broke my concentration. Unless you plan to spend the rest of your life in twelfth grade, I suggest you pay attention!"

The next day I was half-afraid to tell Señorita my decision. I was afraid she'd changed her mind.

"I'm so happy to hear that, Tucker. I know you'll do a good job." I couldn't help but notice that my acceptance brought a change in her tone of voice—more jubilant than soft and flirty.

On Armistice Day I wore a new suit I'd talked Mom into buying. It was charcoal gray flannel. With it I wore a white shirt, buttoned-down collar, and a regimental necktie. Instead of my black Sunday shoes, I wore white bucks. That's how all the college guys were dressed when they came home on weekends. Dirty white bucks were all the rage, and still are. I knew it looked phony, but I didn't care. It made me feel good, like I really was the person I pretended to be, if only for one day.

I stood at attention like a good soldier, and gripped the corners of the podium to stop my shaking. To get into the right spirit, I recalled Mom's story about Uncle Fred going off to war. And as I spoke the words that Señorita had given me to memorize, my eyes got a little teary. I even forgot to be nervous. Looking back, I remember there was a moment of stillness in the auditorium when I finished, and then the room erupted in applause. Applause that washed over me, like a was a movie star, or something! It was the first time in my life I felt proud. Señorita stepped out from behind the curtain and gave me a big hug.

"Tucker, honey, you were wonderful!"

You might think this changed me, that I became more confident, or began to take myself more seriously. But it's not true. I thought of it all as just a fluke, and that the real Tucker Amory was the dumb guy I'd been for so long, and couldn't get used to being anything better. As I said before, it takes a lot to change a person.

Four

"Hey, Tucker, come here, I wanna introduce ya."

It was about midnight Saturday, and I was on my way home from the movies, alone as usual and feeling pretty glum. Bobby Baseborn, one of the guys I should've graduated with, called out to me from his front porch. He'd gone away to college, so I was surprised to see him. There was someone with him, but in the shadows I could barely make them out. When I got close, I could see it was a girl. Both wore freshman beanies, blue and gold, I think, with a letter W in front.

"Wancha to meet Gloria Vane, she's from Squirrel Hill!" He said it real proud, like I was supposed to be impressed.

"Ihay," she said, "Ouryay a eryvay andsomehay oungyay anmay, Ucekertay."

"Eahyay," Bobby said. "Ehay siay a opularpay uygay ithway irlsgay."

I knew I was being teased somehow, not just because the words sounded like a foreign language, but because what's-her-name, Gloria, had a look on her face that gave it away, sort of coy and mocking.

"Huh?" was all I could say in my bewilderment; I'm not quick to see when I'm being set up.

"Hatway siay ouryay irlsgay amenay, Uckertay?" Gloria added.

"He atedday a irlgay astlay earyay hattay adhay a adbay eputationray," Bobbie said, laughing so hard he could hardly get it out.

"His face is turning red. You'd better tell Tucker what's up. You won't run off, now, will you, Tucker?"

She was right. I don't like to be teased, especially when it comes from someone arrogant and stuck on herself. But she was pretty, I could see that; even in the dark she had a nice figure and blonde hair that shone in the moonlight.

"It's pig latin," Bobby said. "You put the front letter on the back of the word and add ay, like you'd say cramsay the ointjay. Ya got it? Pretty clever, uh?"

"Yeah, I guess so," I said, with no enthusiasm.

"Gloria had to learn it for her Chi O initiation. All the pledges had to learn it."

"Uh huh," I said.

"Tucker, you really bug me! How can you be so rude! It's no wonder you—you—"

"I knew what he was about to say, and I was about to tell him to go to hell. Changing her tone, Gloria interrupted and said, "I merely asked if you have a girl friend, Tucker. Do you?"

"Tucker's always got a girl friend. Who is it this year? There've been so many I forget their names."

"I bet Tucker's a great lover," Miss Squirrel Hill said.

"Yeah, he'll father a whole bunch of bastards before we graduate," Bobby chimed in.

This was all I could take from these two. "Time for me to cramsay the ointjay, like you say," and I took off, just as Bobby whispered something to Gloria that made her snicker.

I have to admit, I envied them. Being in college, living in a dorm, meeting new people, even if she was a snooty girl from some ritzy sounding Pittsburgh suburb. College sounded exciting, and they seemed so happy. It made me even more depressed.

On the subject of girls, I have to say I was always in love with somebody in high school. And even in grade school I always had a secret crush. I don't say this because I think I'm hot stuff. It's just that girl friends filled the emptiness. The relationships were always superficial, naturally. I never got really close with any girl. There was never any telling secrets between us. Only one girl tried to get close, and I split with her because she crowded me.

The first girl in my life was not someone I chose. She was the daughter of Mom's best friend. Our moms took us on picnics and tried to pair us up. We were only ten years old. Cathy Clinger was her name. One day at an amusement park our moms shoved us into one of those booths that take instant photos. You know, where if you sit two on a bench you're practically on top of each other. You put a quarter in a slot, and the light flashes, and after you've waited a couple of minutes out come a strip of postage stamp size photos from a watery spout. Our moms thought it real cute, our heads touching and lips smiling so sweet and innocent. I guess I got hooked on that matchmaking. One day I found Mom's wedding ring on her dresser, and I gave it to Cathy. She knew it hadn't come from a five and dime or a Crackerjack box. Her mom recognized it right away and returned it. But I didn't catch hell or anything, though, because Mom was glad I was hooked on Cathy.

Cathy is older now and filled out. I mean she has good breasts, a narrow waist and long legs. Not too long ago, when I got in from school one afternoon, Mom was giving her a new hairdo in the bedroom. Cathy had a towel wrapped around her shoulders and didn't seem to be wearing anything but a bra under it, which was no big deal, except that she was sitting on a bench with only a pair of panties covering her ass. Neither of them showed any concern about me standing there staring at Cathy Clinger's pink panties. So I lingered. Casually, as if I hadn't noticed a thing, I leaned nonchalantly against the door jam and chatted away about any little thing I could think of. I suggested a way Cathy might part her hair. I showed real interest in that! And what color lipstick was best. I had lots to say about that, too! I really wasn't interested so much in staring at Cathy in her pink panties as I was curious to see how long they'd let me stand there. But neither Mom nor Cathy said a word. So I stood there and stared.

Pairing us up when we were little kids was okay, but this seemed a little out of line. Even a horny teenager like me could see that. And then a few days later something else happened, but this time there were no parents in on it.

I gave Cathy a ride home one night in Grandmom's car after a dance. "Tucker," she said, right out of the blue, "take me to Hogback Hollow." This was an unpaved back country road where couples parked, and did it. I knew Cathy didn't really want to do it, she was just a tease. I don't know what she thought we were going to do when we got there. So what I did was I made her think I was taking her to Hogback. On the way we stopped at a red light on a busy street. We could be seen, so I put my arms around her, kissed her real serious-like and slid my hand inside her blouse. She tried to pull away, but I held on till the light turned green, cars behind us honked their horns, and people on the sidewalk started to laugh. Mom's friend still comes to the house, but Cathy stays away.

My first real girl friend was Sally Tears. She was a blue-eyed blond who played French horn in the marching band. We were introduced one summer at a friend's house. I could tell she liked me because she directed all her attention at me the whole time. One reason I fell for her was she was sitting across from me, wearing tight shorts. She had her knees drawn up, and I could see the hem of her panties peeking out. She posed like that often. Even when she wore a skirt, she often sat so that I could see more than most girls would show. Not that she was a bad girl. Maybe she just did it unconsciously. We necked and had some pretty hot times, but I never tried to go too far. I was too timid.

We went together only a few months. It was because I got bored. She cried a lot when we broke up. She even followed me around and used her friends to try to get me back. That was a new experience for me; it was usually the girl who dumped me. Altogether, I went with seven different girls in high school. I don't say this to brag. It's like I said before: I had to have a girl in my life. It made me feel good about myself. Girls didn't care whether you could catch a football or get good grades.

Most were good girls. We'd have fun times at amusement parks, movies, or just sit around and chat. Good girls always seem to have large families, and you spend a lot of time hanging around the house, talking with parents, brothers and sisters, and you're seldom left alone together. You spend the time playing monopoly or something. You drink lemonade, kiss good-bye, and you go home feeling good because you had a good time.

Then there was Joan Dark. She came from a big Catholic family. I don't know how we got to dating. We'd grown up in the same neighborhood and played together, and then in high school we just sort of fell into it. It couldn't have been her looks that got me; she was a little plump and had acne real bad. She was an honor student and a member of all the important clubs and committees. But we never talked about school, though. She knew it was not my favorite subject of conversation.

Once she asked me to go to Sunday night mass with her. I'd walked past her church, St. Joe's, many times. I liked to peek through the high arched door at the worshippers. Once I thought I saw brilliant gold light and smelled incense. There were pale-faced nuns swishing around in black habits, with heavy gold chains swinging from their waists. The priests wore long black skirts and hats with Mickey Mouse ears. They all seemed to be holy and unapproachable, like they were saints. I was intrigued, so I agreed to go.

It was dark when Joan and I reached the church. Worshippers were hurrying in, mostly old folks, dressed in blue and black and brown, the women's heads covered with black lace doilies. Inside, the church was what I imagined it to be, and more: a brilliance of gold light shining out from the altar; heavily painted plaster saints wearing lipstick; richly woven tapestries and curtains; gold cups and crosses; and an enormous blood-stained crucifix towering over it all from the domed ceiling, like nothing I'd ever seen before. Like it was Heaven, or something. Along the side walls stood several little altars. When I saw a big blaze in front of one of them, I got scared, thinking the place was on fire. But it was just candles. And there were confessionals, like the ones I'd seen in movies. For a moment I got real nervous. I whispered my fear to Joan, but she just laughed and whispered back that she just knew I had probably saved up a lot to confess about. There was a strong odor in the air that seemed to be everywhere. It was incense. St. Joe's was an old church, and I figured it must have seeped into every corner and crevice over the years. The richness of it all; the heavy golden light, and the solemn chant in Latin sung by the priests when the mass started was a little too much for me, and I was glad when it was over.

Everything about Joan Dark—her big family, her brilliant mind, and her heavy religion were all too rich for me. I guess that's why we split up. Like Huck Finn in the novel, when he said the Grangerfords he stayed with gave him the fantods.

I guess you could say I was preoccupied with girls. Being with girls gave me some of the best and the worst times I had all through high school. Girls who were hard to win became an obsession. Any girl who wasn't, I dropped pretty soon. Of course, I got dropped by some of them, and it really shook me up. Good girls, as I said, were fun to be with; there were never any arguments or frustrations. Bad girls gave me worries and made me feel bad about myself. But I always preferred the bad girls, because they made me feel alive. There must be something wrong when you have to feel bad to feel alive.

Actually, though, there was only one bad girl in my life. Leila Moore was her name. Like me, her parents were separated and she lived with her grandparents. They lived in a big house about a hundred years old. It had turrets and spires and tall windows. But her grandparents didn't occupy the whole house, just an apartment in the back. You had to walk down a long, dark hall to get to it. I remember this hall because something funny happened on a date one night just as Leila and I were leaving. Leila stopped suddenly, turned around and raced back to the apartment. She didn't tell me what had happened till later in the evening: her panties had started to fall down, and she had to change.

Leila's grandparents were old-fashioned and aloof. Whenever I called for her, they'd say hello in an owlish kind of way, "Helloooo," and then they'd leave the room, like they were afraid of me. They let Leila do pretty much as she pleased. We spent many long nights necking and petting on the living room sofa, almost till dawn, sometimes. She taught me to French kiss and pet and get pretty hot. But you know, we never went too far, probably because I was too scared.

Sometimes we spent evenings at her best friend's house, who happened to be my cousin. They were super bridge players. While they played with partners, I watched. I never learned the game, partly because it bored me and partly because they were too advanced to be bothered teaching me. The reason I mention this is because bridge had something to do with Leila and me breaking up.

One night I phoned her about going out. She hesitated. There was just something about the tone of her voice that tipped me off. "I, uh, can't tonight, Tucker, my grandma needs me at home. Her back's bothering her again."

I knew this was a lie: her grandmother's back troubles never stopped her from doing as she pleased. And this wasn't the only fault I'd seen in her, or the first time I was suspicious. So what happened was, I pretended to believe her. After I hung up, I phoned some of the guys I'd begun to hang out with, to see what was up with them. When we assembled outside Rogan's Dairy and were inhaling our weeds, I mentioned my doubts about how Leila was spending her evening. "I've got a hunch," Bill Miller said. "Let's drop by your cousin's." Sure enough, there she was. The card table was set up on a screened-in side porch. From behind the shrubs we could see everything. Leila's bridge partner was a guy I'd seen giving her the eye at teen dances.

Bill suddenly got this great idea. For about a year, he'd been carrying a condom in his wallet. A Trojan, I think. He'd carried it so long it had made a permanent impression in the leather. He peeled off the foil wrapper and passed it around, and we all spat into it. Then he tiptoed over to Bridge Partner's car parked in front of the house, opened the passenger side door and tossed it onto the seat. Saliva oozed out and made a little puddle on the cloth upholstery. The car was a brand new Chevy two-door, gray, with an awning over the windshield and a little prism on the dash so the driver could see red lights overhead. It was a school night, it was getting late, and we knew the game would break up soon. So we waited in the shrubbery. It was October, it was cool, and dry leaves scattered on the ground gave off a prickly sort of light under the street lamps. The little prism on the Chevy's dash glowed like a mischievous eye.

We didn't have to wait long. Laughing and teasing, they ran down the sidewalk. Bridge Partner opened the car door for Leila, and she slid across the seat so she could cuddle up to him. By the time he got around to his side, Leila knew she'd sat in something wet. And then she discovered what it was. Boy, did she scream! "God damn it, what have you done to me? I'm gonna be pregnant!"

Bridge Partner, voice shaking, stuttered, "Jesus, Leila, yer gonna be heard all over the neighborhood. Will ya shut up!" With a pocket hanky he tried to scrub the spot dry, and then reached out to wipe Leila's skirt.

"Don't touch me with that! Just get me home, you bastard!"

Bridge partner's car peeled away from the curb. We all watched till his tail lights disappeared around a corner, and then broke into hysterics.

Later, when I got home and went to bed I couldn't sleep, knowing that someone would tell Leila what we'd done.

And I was right. In the hall next day in school she kept her distance, her eyes full of scorn and hatred.

That was the end of that relationship. In a way I was glad it was over, and it was several months before I started dating again. As I look back on it, I can say I was happier when I didn't have a steady girl. I felt free and less anxious.

Five

"Tucker, are you ready to recite?" she asked, thumping her wooden leg on the floor in anger.

It was Peg Leg, my English teacher. Each of us had to go up front, stand beside her and recite from memory a poem in our literature book. I hadn't done it because there was no poem in the book I wanted to memorize. It was all stupid, sentimental crap, like "Casey at the Bat," which all the so-called athletes shot their wad over, and Kipling's "If", which all the girls swooned over, pretending it was so morally "uplifting."

The worst part of it was, when each guy or girl went up front to recite, Peg Leg had the book open on the desk where she was sitting, and all any kid had to do was look down and read it off the page, which was what everyone was doing. She never caught anyone doing it. But with my luck I'd have been the one who got caught. Anyway, the whole thing was pretty stupid.

"No, I'm not!" I yelled back.

"This is the third time this week I've called on you! When *will* you be ready?"

"Never!" I yelled.

She sure as hell heard the irritation in my voice. "Tucker Amory, I've had enough of your insolence! Report to Mr. Feralman immediately!"

Peg Leg is Miss Kimm, a little spinster about four feet eleven. Her hair's bobbed and hangs in bangs. No one seems to know how she got her wooden leg, and no one asks or pokes fun because she's a popular teacher, with the brown-nosers, that is. But she and I don't get along, probably because I don't suck up to her.

I'm not really a hell-raiser. That is, I don't see myself that way. I don't try to make trouble or draw attention to myself, the way some guys do. Usually, when I'm frustrated or anxious, I shut down rather than act up. And I'm not insolent, but she got me going.

Because Feralman had called me into his office the day before, when I got caught skipping gym, I didn't want to show up there again so soon, so I walked the halls for a while. I knew I couldn't be seen in the halls for very long, what with the tight rules and all, so I ducked into a boys room, took down my pants and sat on a toilet. And there I stayed, for about half an hour. When the dismissal bell rang, ending English period, my ass was pretty damn cold.

All the rest of the day I expected to receive a summons, but none came. After school I didn't go home right away, figuring Feralman would've called Mom. But when I got home at supper time, Mom said nothing.

In homeroom next day, and all through first and second period, I sweated it out. But no summons came. And then it was time for English. If I'd gone to class, Peg Leg would've asked for an admission slip. If I'd gone instead to Feralman's office, a day late, I'd have been in double trouble. I couldn't decide what to do, so I went back to the boys room and sat on a toilet again. Half way through the period a teacher came in, tried the handle, and peeked into my stall. Maybe he suspected me of smoking, like some teachers who make a career of catching smokers. They spend more time darting into boys rooms than teaching classes. Satisfied I wasn't breaking any rules, he left. And so I sat out another period. Again that day, I sweated out a summons. None came.

On the third day, I was seated on the same damn toilet, in the same damn boys room, when in came the same damn teacher who had seen me the day before. I decided I'd have to find somewhere else to hide. Besides, I'd been walking around all day smelling like toilet disinfectant. The morning of the fourth day came, and still no summons. I ducked into the boys room, waited till the halls cleared, and then stepped into the library next door, figuring Red, the librarian, would think I'd just come from a study hall. Red looked at the clock and frowned, but didn't say anything, and I was able to take a seat without having to explain myself.

I'd never visited the school library before. I could see it was about the size of two classrooms, if you placed them end to end. One wall was all windows, the other three all covered with book shelves from the floor almost to the ceiling. The wood floor was bare and creaky. The trim around doors and windows painted pukey green. And the books smelled musty.

I couldn't just sit and do nothing, Red would've gotten wise to that, so I grabbed a book off a shelf, the first one my eyes settled on. It was a biography of General Eisenhower, the kind that makes its subject a big fat hero with no faults.

During English period every day, I hid in the library and read. I behaved myself and smiled sweetly to Red, so she wouldn't suspect. One day I picked a book of stories by Nathaniel Hawthorne, attracted to it by the cover that showed a picture of ghosts. One story in particular stood out because it was really strange. It was called "Rappaccini's Daughter".

There's this old guy who has a daughter he sort of keeps hidden in a magical garden. A young guy falls in love with her, but he doesn't know she's enchanted, her dad having done something to her to make her poisonous. To tell the truth, I know girls like that—strictly poison! They think they've got something magical about them, but when you get too close, they get venomous. Anyway, what happens is, the young guy discovers he's become poisonous, too, from having been with her in the garden. He buys a bouquet of flowers for her, but when he breathes on them they all die. In the end the young guy gives the girl a herb-like drink that's supposed to destroy evil, but ends up killing the girl. I suppose that's supposed to mean something, but I couldn't make it out. I liked the story, anyway.

I'd always liked reading, when I could choose my own books, and now I found that books helped me forget my troubles. Next I read an adventure called *Redburn*, about a young sailor growing up in the 1800s. It was pretty good, too. One day I stopped in front of the philosophy section. There was this ancient Greek named Plato. I'd heard the name somewhere and I was curious. Plato, I discovered, had some pretty interesting ideas about truth, beauty, and goodness: that they are absolutes, and what we experience in real life is just a small part of what they are in their purest form, somewhere off in the absolute, which was pretty neat. But the philosophers who really got to me were the guys who had practical ideas. Like William James, for instance. Unlike the preachers who tell you to have faith because if you don't you'll burn in hell, he said people should have faith because faith can make good things happen. If you believe something's possible, you can make it happen, and he told a lot of stories about how ordinary people actually did make good things happen through faith. I liked that. And then there was Einstein, the mathematician and deep thinker. He said he didn't believe in a personal god, which made sense to me. He said there was a creator and described him as "the rational force that is made manifest in the universe," and to find god is to find that which unifies all the forces of nature. And he said that "science without religion is lame, religion without science is blind." For a guy whose ideas about science baffle a lot of ordinary folks, he sure made sense to me when it came to religion. The philosophers who made the greatest impression on me were the existentialists. They believe that you create what you are, and all the crap about original sin is just a lot of bull. They say there are no rules about the meaning of life, except the ones we create ourselves. I liked that idea, too. One day I turned to a guy sitting beside me at my table and whispered, "Did you know that existence precedes essence?" Ha! Ha! You should have seen the look on his face. He must've thought I was crazy, or something, because he got up and moved to another table.

Four weeks went by, and still no summons. I figured Peg Leg must have forgotten about me, and she must not have told Feralman about tossing me out. I knew the longer this went on the worse my punishment would be, but I just couldn't turn myself in.

One day, just as I was taking my seat at the beginning of the period, Red motioned for me to come to the charge desk. This is it, I thought, they've finally caught up with me!

"Tucker, you certainly are an avid reader. I'm very impressed with the kind of books you read. Your English teacher must be very proud of you."

"Uh, yeah," I said.

"Would you like to be a library aide? I have no one to work this period. I need someone to shelve books and do odd jobs in the storage room. You'd get to wear a worm badge pinned to your shirt. You'd have something to show off to your classmates!"

"Worm badge?"

"You'd be one of Miss Toomey's book worms!" She smiled proudly, like this was some kind of honor.

How could I refuse? Four weeks and I'd spent every third period in the library. I couldn't say no and continue to show up every day. There was nowhere else to hide, so I said yes.

Red, Miss Toomey, that is, was to me an odd-looking woman. She was about Mom's age. She had bright red, almost orange, hair that stuck out in curls like Little Orphan Annie. Her skin was very pale, almost transparent. She wore fire engine red lipstick and favored satiny green and purple blouses, which were just a little too tight. Some of the girls who came into the library whispered about her. They said she was love-starved and all her "worms" were guys.

Miss Toomey and I got along pretty well. I did everything she asked and never goofed-off, because I liked the work and had first choice of all the new books.

Things were going along just fine, and I almost forgot about English, until one day I walked into the library at the usual time. There was Feralman—standing at the charge desk.

"Tucker, Mr. Feralman wants to talk to you privately, in the storage room." Her face had turned red like her hair, and she spoke kind of out of breath.

Feralman sat on the work table, but left me standing. He was wearing his gray suit. He owned only two suits, which he wore a week at a time. This was gray week, next week would be blue. The pants of both had shiny seats. The room was very dusty, and he sneezed a few times before he started in on me. From the inside pocket of his coat, he pulled out a report card. Very slowly and menacing, enjoying the moment, he said, "I suppose you know that report cards came out today."

"Not really." I said. I don't know why I gave such a dumb answer. Maybe I felt I was being drawn into a trap.

"What grade do you expect to receive in English?"

"I don't know."

My evasive answers made him so angry his neck began to swell, and for a moment I thought the knot in his necktie would break, seeing as how his collars were too tight, even when he wasn't angry.

He threw his arms above his head in a mock display of exasperation, leaped off the table as dramatically as he could and ordered me to follow him to his office. By the time we got there, he had calmed down. While he did a few slow turns in his swivel chair, his mind working over what to do with me, I watched the minute hand of his wall clock do a few rotations. Saying nothing he scribbled some words on an admission slip and ordered me back to my long-abandoned English class.

No tongue-lashing! No suspension! Not even after-school detention! When I handed Peg Leg my admission slip, she didn't look at me or say a word, only indicated I should take my assigned seat. Classmates gawked in amazement. Many thought I'd been shipped off to another class, which is what I had told those who asked.

Why hadn't I been punished? It had to be that both Peg Leg and Feralman were too embarrassed to make a big deal about it all. For sure, they couldn't call my mom, or their negligence would be revealed.

A week passed. As much as I tried not to let it bother me, I couldn't help feeling guilty about deceiving Miss Toomey. She'd been kind to me, and I felt I owed her an apology. I had some books to return, so one day I went to see her.

"I've been wondering if I'd ever see you again," she said, coolly.

"I'm sorry I let you down, Miss Toomey. I should have been honest with you about third period."

"You disappointed me, Tucker. I had such a high opinion of you. You certainly know how to fool a person."

"I know it was a dumb thing to do. I don't know why I let it go on for such a long time. I do crazy things sometimes that I know I'll have to pay a price for sooner or later, but I do them, anyway. It's like I'm hypnotized and can't help it."

"Tucker, I don't understand you, and I can't help you. You embarrassed me. What must Mr. Feralman think? Probably that I was your conspirator." Her face turned red, like her hair. "Don't you ever come into this library again!"

Miss Toomey had never lashed out at me before, and it really hurt to hear her say this. My face flushed with shame and anger, I ran back to study hall, collapsed in my seat and put my head down on my desk, so no one would see how upset I was. It was the same old story I got from my parents and teachers—all they seemed to care about was how I'd upset *them*, and how hurt *they* were!

I stayed home the next day, telling Mom I had an earache. Ever since the ear trouble I'd had in first grade, this excuse worked. With nothing to do all day, I thought about some of the books I'd read in the library, and then I remembered I still had a library book, a book of poetry. I don't know why I signed it out; poetry is what first got me into trouble. Kind of indifferent, I searched for it and found it among the stuff on a shelf that held my junk. I fanned the pages and was just about to toss it aside, when a title caught my eye. It was "Chicago," a poem by Carl Sandburg. It caught my eye because Chicago had been my home for three years during the war, and I was curious. Here's how it went:

Hog Butcher for the world,
Tool Maker, Stacker of Wheat
Player with railroads, and the Nation's
  Freight Handler.
Stormy, husky, brawling
City of the Big Shoulders...

"Wow!" I said to myself, "that's pretty neat!" The words were strong and manly, not at all like the swishy stuff we were forced to read in English class. So I read it again, this time out loud. Mom heard me and came into the living room, a needle and thread in one hand and the sleeve of a dress in the other.

"What's that you're reading, Tucker?" Ever since I'd started bringing home books, she'd taken an interest, or maybe I should say suspicion.

"Doesn't this sound just like Chicago, Mom?" I read a few more lines out loud.

"It certainly sounds like Chicago to me—smelly and dirty and full of undesirable people. But it doesn't make me feel anything. And it doesn't rhyme, does it? Poetry's supposed to rhyme." And with that she went back to her sewing, making little scratching sounds with her thimble.

There were several more poems about Chicago, and one that had a cat in it. It sounded kind of soft, and I thought Mom might like it, so I took it to her and read it aloud:

The fog comes
on little cat feet.

It sits looking
over harbor and city
on silent haunches
and then moves on.

After I read it, there was a pause. I thought maybe she hadn't heard me. "Well, what did you think of that?"

"It's all right," she said. "Is that all there is to it? How can you call that a poem?"

I was really disappointed. She's always telling me I should get "cultured", but she doesn't appreciate my idea of culture. I had never before experienced what the poems in that book did to me—every word a clear picture of the city I remembered, but thought I'd forgotten. It was the first time anything artsy seemed to reflect real life.

This made me want to read more. I especially liked the poems of Edwin Arlington Robinson and Edgar Lee Masters. (It's funny how some poets like to sign their poems with three names.) There was a guy in a poem named Richard Corey, who everybody in his town thought he was real happy, until one night he went home and blew his head off; and Miniver Cheevy, who wept, regretting he was ever born. Boy, I knew how that felt! I'd always been taught that poems had to be about big heroes who seldom did anything wrong, and that poems taught you to be good and true. But these poems were about reality.

Then this idea came to me: maybe I could write poems. I got paper and pencil and made a list of people and places I could write about. There was old Mr. Ramsey, who was a kindly neighbor when I was little. He had no children of his own, so he sort of adopted us kids in the neighborhood. He gave us candy, and on hot summer days let us run barefoot under the water fountain in his back yard, so I wrote a poem thanking him. I wrote a poem for Miss Quack, the grade school principal who let me move up to second grade, even though I'd flunked first. Another nice thing about her was, if a kid was coming late for school, and she'd see him running through the field, out of breath, hoping to beat the tardy bell, she'd hold it till he got there. The poem goes like this:

THE PRINCIPAL

A few years ago this school,
two stories of red brick,
crowning a knoll, stood like an island
in a sea of tall grass.

We kids entered by a flight
of concrete steps, as if climbing
into church or court.
Today, new brick houses

float around it like buoys with no bells.
In the shadows of our memories,
you are standing at the top of the steps

like a nun or a judge,
waiting for late boys and girls,
to ring the tardy bell. We run past you
and step noisily into the cool, dark corridor.

You shut the outer door.
Bang, it went against our tardiness!
Inside, where we always felt like sinners
or culprits, you tried to save us
from hell or hanging, but failed.

We stand in shadows now,
where the path vanished,
where tall green grass stood above us,
where new houses now block our view,
the little kid in us still needing you.

When I think about it, I wonder if I didn't learn more about literature outside English class than in it. I even had this idea about letting my hair grow long, buying a tweed coat and a pipe, and becoming a poet. I wanted to know if that poem was any good, so after I returned to English class, I showed it to Peg Leg, but she ridiculed it. So I quit writing poems.

Six

All day rain had pelted the windows of my classes and made puddles on the sills. Now it was late afternoon in Sales and Merchandising class, and I was pasting cut-out magazine ads onto posterboard. It was a project The Rock had assigned. (This was what we called Mr. Rockapalumbo for short.)

We were supposed to be learning about advertising. Just for the hell of it, I'd cut out lingerie ads, the real sexy kind. The guys made dirty gestures and the girls giggled, but The Rock about had a stroke over it. Just then the dismissal bell rang, and a cheer went up. I stashed my cutouts in a storage closet and raced back to homeroom. Old Gussie was smiling for once, and wishing everybody, "Happy Thanksgiving! May your turkey be tender and juicy," as we ran into the hall and scrambled for the exits.

I turned up my collar against the rain. Girls, doing their usual act to attract guys' attention, screamed about their hair getting wet, and guys reached down, scooped handfuls of water and tossed them at the girls and each other. Dodging puddles and not looking where I was going, I ran the half block to Grandmom's house. Just before I got there, something pink caught my eye and pulled me up short—it was Dad's car parked in front. His brand new coral pink 1950 Kaiser, which the last time he came had attracted a lot of attention. Kaisers were not quite in Coaltown's league yet. To me it looked like a pink wiener on wheels, or like the silly cars you see in cartoons.

My shoulders tightened. I opened the front door, and there he was, seated in the big chair facing the door. As usual there was no hug or handshake, just a cold hello. He gave me a quick once-over, and seeing nothing to jump on, turned away. I considered telling him about S. and M. class, which I thought might earn a few brownie points, considering he was a salesman. But I didn't want him to know anything that was going on with me—it would have meant opening myself up.

He stayed for dinner. If this had meant he was going to stay the night, it would be at Nanna's, his mother's house.

"He wants to discuss something with you, Tucker," Mom said.

Dad finished chewing on a piece of chopped steak. It must have been tough meat because it took him a long time to swallow it. He touched his napkin to his mouth, doing it so slowly and deliberately, like maybe his mouth was bleeding, or something. "Would you like to go to Chicago with me next week? It would give us a chance to talk man to man and you could look up all your old playmates. We would leave on Thursday. I'd take care of my business on Friday, and we would return on the weekend. You'd miss only two days of school."

I guess I was supposed to be relieved, knowing I'd miss only two days of school.

"It's a chance for you to spend some time with your father," Mom said. "Heaven knows where you'll be next year. My friends say, once children go away to college, they hardly ever see them again." And she let out a little sigh.

I wanted to say—that's assuming I'll graduate, that I'll go away to college, and that I want to spend some time with my dad.

The years we lived in Chicago during the war were the happiest years of my childhood, and I wanted to make this trip, even if it meant spending many long boring hours in the car with him. Chicago was a day's journey, and another day back, more time than I'd ever spent with him during my whole life! But I really wanted to visit the old neighborhood again and see my old playmates. How much bigger they'd be now, and older!

After a night at Nanna's house, he ate Thanksgiving dinner, and for the umpteenth time while we ate, we had to listen to the story of Nanna's family and how it was descended from Mayflower Pilgrim John Howland, and we should remember the Pilgrims on this day and be grateful. But I just couldn't be grateful to someone I didn't know, who died a couple hundred years ago. Dad left soon after pumpkin pie, which we almost didn't have because Grandmom set it on a window sill to cool, and it fell into the snow outside.

Anticipation made the next week go by very slowly. I knew without asking that he would come to town the night before, without announcing his arrival, and stay the night at Nanna's. And sure enough, when the day came, the bleak November morning was lit up by the appearance of Dad's pink Kaiser, all gassed up and ready to go. I kissed Mom good-bye, dropped my stuff in the trunk, and climbed in. Mom waved good-bye, teary-eyed.

It wasn't long before the hills of Pennsylvania fell behind us, and the flat farm land of Ohio stretched out in front. Cleveland was two hours away, Toledo another two hours, then Indiana, and finally Chicago at the end of the day.

We cruised along, and the hum of the wheels lulled me into a kind of stupor. I waited for him to say something—whatever it was we were supposed to talk about, man to man. But there was only small talk—how much mileage the Kaiser got per gallon and how dreary the weather. In half an hour we reached Youngstown. Soon the Cleveland skyline would come into view.

On the seat beside me, I found catalogs and price lists. Dad was in commercial refrigeration now. Artists' renderings of dairy showcases, walk-in freezers, cross section views of insulation, electrical grids. All pretty boring stuff. I picked up a catalog and leafed through it, thinking he might take the cue and tell me about his work. But he said nothing, and I didn't ask. So I turned on the radio. Nothing but women's programs: phony-sounding voices reading recipes for casseroles and desserts, and advice for the lovelorn. I shut it off. We were on the outskirts of Cleveland now, and still nothing from him—nothing but the hum of the motor and the monotony of the road.

"What was the name of the girl you had a crush on?" he asked, suddenly, jolting me out of a mid-morning nap.

I stretched, yawned, and stewed over who he was talking about. "I suppose you mean Diane Fair."

"Yes. Do you ever hear from her?"

"We traded letters for a while," I said, pretending indifference. "Her family moved out of the neighborhood, but I have her new address."

"What was your friend's name, the one whose older brother was an Army Air Corps pilot?"

"Emil," I said. Emil Opitz was my best friend in Chicago. His brother gave us Army Air Corps brass emblems to wear on our shirts and caps when we played

Flying Tigers. What possible interest could he have in my friends? When we lived in Chicago during the war, he never even looked in their direction, never asked how I was doing in school, and never asked what was going on in any part of my life. So I volunteered nothing now.

Between Cleveland and Toledo there was nothing to look at but lonely, flat stretches of farmland shivering in the cold, so I slid down in my seat, lay my head back and daydreamed about the three years I'd lived in Chicago, as I said before, the happiest years of my childhood.

It all began on December 7, 1941, with the announcement on radio that Pearl Harbor had been bombed by the Japanese.

A dark, dreary Sunday afternoon. Grandmom's house full of Sunday stillness. Grandmom listening intently to her radio. Mom not at home. I stand a few feet away, staring at the radio, a little plastic box, ivory, with lighted yellow dial. The announcer, excited, is recalling the terrible events as they happened—all about a cowardly attack by Japanese carrier-based aircraft, bombing and strafing helpless soldiers and civilians, and sinking a fleet of warships anchored unsuspectingly in the waters of Pearl Harbor. The attack had come in the early morning hours when crews were asleep. I listen in wonder and ask myself how could such shocking news come from a little plastic container of vacuum tubes and wires no bigger than my grade school lunch box. Grandmom shakes her head sadly, "I remember the day in 1917. Your Uncle Fred left home to fight in France. He was gassed, you know, and has suffered sick lungs ever since." She paused. "And you," she said, "are too young to go to war!" Does she really think I'd try to enlist at age ten?

June 1942. The war in the Pacific is all anyone talks about. Mom calls it war fever. I am eleven. Mom and I board a train, the same train I used to cycle downtown to watch make its morning arrival from New York City, roaring into the station belching steam, its bell clanging a warning to stay off the tracks, its high windows crowded with strangers I'd probably never see again. Always different yet always the same. When we lived in New York, Mom and I frequently rode this train to and fro. But now we are on our way to Chicago. Mom's wearing a summer suit, man-style, light gray with pin stripes. She designed it and cut the pattern herself. The jacket has lapels and padded shoulders and buttons tightly at the waist. Her hair's rolled back behind her ears. Her hat has feathers poking out on the side of her head. She designed it too. I wear white flannel trousers, white dress shirt and tie, and a yacht cap, tilted so far forward I have to keep my head back to see where I'm going. It's my mock Navy officer's uniform.

In a Pullman car we find our berth. It has soft upholstered seats surrounded by richly grained wood paneling. I know from past trips that our bench-type seats facing each other roll together to form a bed at night, when a Negro porter comes to prepare the car for all-night travel, and the same for an upper berth above that swings down to form another bed. There will be crisp white sheets and warm wool blankets, and heavy black curtains to give us privacy. The gently rolling motion of the train and the clicking of the wheels will lull me to sleep, when I lie down a few miles out of Coaltown and wake up in Chicago.

The conductor cries, "All aboard," and the train announces its departure with a shudder of its couplings. An hour later, a waiter from the dining car passes down the aisle tapping a dinner gong.

The dining car is all starched white table cloths, heavy silver dinnerware, and Negro waiters in starched white coats carrying huge trays of food that give off wonderful smells of steak and potatoes, fish and vegetables, wines, pies, and hot coffee; on each table a crystal bud vase holding a single red rose; each window trimmed in gold-fringed curtains. I order steak and potatoes, Mom something French.

Back in our berth, I press my face to the window, peer into the night, barely able to make out the dark shapes of towns and villages, cities with factories and warehouses and slums—the only parts of cities that trains pass through. The porter comes and makes our beds, Mom below and me in the upper berth. He dims the lights in the aisle, and the Pullman car grows quiet.

I awake to daylight and the train chugging into Randolph Station. Dad is there to meet us. We pile into a yellow taxi, its rear window open and a little canvas awning hanging oddly over the trunk.

We arrive at our new home, an apartment on the South Side. Jackson Park is nearby and Lake Michigan. Our building is an apartment hotel, with richly furnished suites. The management provides linens, cooking utensils, and twice-a-week maid service. Dad, a mechanical engineer, can afford this luxury because he's boss of a construction job, putting up a new mill for Republic Steel.

The streets of Chicago are full of uniformed men: soldiers, sailors, marines. Lots of sailors because the Great Lakes Naval Training Station is just up the coast of Lake Michigan. Sometimes I sit in the living room bay window of our twentieth floor apartment and gaze in awe at U.S. Navy fighter planes practicing dog fights over the lake—looping, diving, swooping dangerously around each other, just like in the war movies.

I make new friends and playmates. The war fills our play-time hours. Boy scout uniforms become army khakis. We tote toy MI rifles bought at Woolworths and dig fox holes in a nearby vacant lot.

John Wayne war movies fill our Saturday afternoons with excitement. Our playtime afterwards reflects whatever movie we see. Movies of the war in Europe have us fighting Nazis; movies of the war in the air have us turning living room furniture into imaginary P-41s or B-17s. We trade Army or Air Corps shoulder patches the way we had done with baseball cards before the war.

These are the happiest years of my childhood. Mom and Dad are together. I do okay in school. I have lots of friends and playmates. I even have a girl friend who thinks I'm something special. And great events happen daily in the big city that surrounds me.

In September I enter sixth grade at Parkside Elementary, just around the corner from our apartment building. How different it is from school in Coaltown. The teachers hardly ever tell us what to do. We are encouraged to follow our interests, but we have to do something constructive, like reading or writing. I like to read, so I spend some time in the library. Jimmy Margolis likes to draw, mostly war scenes, so he spends his time in the art room. Sometimes the teachers call us together and teach something they think we ought to know, like arithmetic and such. But even this is different. The teacher thinks we should know geometry, so she gives each of us a ruler and compass, explains what a right angle is and tells us to figure out how to bisect it, using the tools she gave us. No rule is ever explained. We have to figure everything out for ourselves. The teacher turns it into a game, to see who makes the first discovery or gets a correct answer. Sometimes I am first. We never get homework, and nothing we do is ever given a grade. In fact, we never get report cards. I don't know how Mom and Dad keep track of my progress. Nothing ever happens to make me anxious. There are times when Dad doesn't come home for several days, but Mom seems to tolerate his absences, and I do, too. Only once does it bother me. It's a Saturday and my birthday, and Mom takes me shopping at Marshall Fields for a birthday gift. We have lunch in a fancy restaurant. I think Dad will be waiting when we get home, but the apartment is dark. Mom and I eat cake and ice cream, and I go to bed about eleven. Sometime during the night I wake up and hear loud voices. They are at each other over Dad not being home to celebrate my birthday. The next day it doesn't even occur to me to expect a present from him.

Indiana was just as flat and boring as Ohio, but it didn't take long to cross. It was dark when we rolled into Chicago. The apartment buildings looked oddly familiar, like something in a dream, only the dream was memory—all those rows of bay windows looking out in front, and all those porches in back, connected by stairs rising five floors above the alleys.

We checked into a hotel on Stony Island Avenue, not far from the old neighborhood. I couldn't wait. I grabbed the phone in our room and asked the operator to connect me with a number I looked up in the directory. I didn't care about Dad hearing me.

"Hello."

"Is this Diane?"

"Yes, it is."

"This is Tucker, Diane."

"Tucker who?

"You mean there's been more than one Tucker in your life?"

"Tucker! Tucker Amory! Is this really you?" She sure was excited. "Where are you calling from?"

"Here, right here in Chicago, the Stony Island Hotel." I told her about the trip and asked about her family.

"Mom's had female surgery, but she's fine now. Dad and Bruce are just great. Am I going to see you while you're here?"

"Sure, and Bruce, I want to see him too." Bruce was her little brother, five years younger than me. I was kind of a hero to him, but I can't say why.

"Is tomorrow morning okay?"

"What time?"

"Nine o'clock?"

"That's fine. It's a school day, but I'll explain to Mom, and Bruce has a dentist appointment, so he'll be here, too. Oh, Tucker, I can hardly wait to see you! It's been so long. Why did you stop writing? I wrote to your mother once, when I hadn't heard from you, but she didn't answer. I thought you forgot about me." The way she said it put a lump in my throat.

Mom never told me about the letter. She resented Diane, because one time I refused to go shopping. Diane's parents had invited me to go to a movie, and I prefered to go with them. There was a big scene, and Mom accused me of favoring Diane's family over my own, which was true. I remember how guilty I was made to feel, but I stomped out of the apartment and went to the movie, anyway.

"I'm sorry about not writing. I guess I just got out of the habit." This was a lie. I was dating someone at the time, and Diane just faded from my mind.

After hanging up, I was excited. It was too early to go to bed, and I needed someting to do. So I went down to the lobby and found a television lounge. I plopped down in a deep leather chair and watched what was on—a pair of muscle-bound wrestlers doing all kinds of dumb gyrations, the image all blurred by what looked like snow flakes.

We didn't have television at Grandmom's house, nor did anyone else on the block. It was expensive—about two hundred bucks! Unlike radio that had lots of stations, television had only two channels. They came on at eleven a.m. and signed off at midnight. Besides a few sports events, there was *Kukla, Fran and Ollie, Musical Mailbox, Arthur Godfrey,* and not much else.

Back in the room, I was a long time going to sleep. Thinking about Diane kept me awake. How we got to know each other back then, and all.

We'd been living in Chicago only a few weeks. I had seen her often, playing in the next block with her friends.

They always seemed to be chasing each other, playing some kind of tag. One day she looked across and asked if I wanted to play. When I crossed over and got close enough to see her real good, something hit me hard—the most beautiful big brown eyes I'd ever seen! It was some kind of instant recognition—love at first sight. And I could see she felt it too. We were sweethearts from that moment on, until I left Chicago three years later, when Mom and Dad split up again, and Mom and me went to live with Grandmom again back in Coaltown.

After breakfast in the hotel coffee shop, Dad left the car with me while he took a train into the Loop. Traffic was heavy at this time in the morning, but it didn't take long to find the address Diane had given me. She lived on a street of nearly identical little brick bungalows. When I drew up in front, I saw a face in the window. I sat for a moment before I got out of the car. I was suddenly very nervous; it hadn't occured to me that she had probably changed, grown up and all, and I might not recognize her. She would no longer be the twelve-year-old I had left behind in 1945—a head shorter, straight up and down, with tiny breasts just beginning to show.

The front door opened, and there she was—big brown eyes, still shining, still sweet and innocent. But everything else was different. She was exactly my height now, maybe even a little taller, her figure wonderfully curvy under a white angora sweater. Both of us, I think, had the same first impression: "I didn't know what to expect, and I wasn't prepared for this!"

She spoke first. "Like I said on the phone, my parents aren't here, but Bruce will be back soon."

We sat facing each other, she on a big, thick upholstered chair and me on a matching sofa, furniture I didn't recognize. A funny feeling came over me, like I was half in and half out of this world, or like I was in a dream world. I guess that's what happens when you step back into a memory and some of what was fixed there in time suddenly becomes new and changed, like a movie when the story suddenly jumps way ahead in time.

"Is any of the old gang still around?"

She seemed surprised by the question. "I don't know, Tucker. I haven't been to Kregier Avenue in ages. Everything changed after the war. You moved away, and gradually everybody else, too. I think some of the families moved to the suburbs."

I was really surprised at how hard this news hit me. I had hoped to see Emil, and Arnold, and Billy, and all the kids I had played with. "You've not heard from any of them?"

"No," she said, a little impatiently, and I could see her memories of those times were not very important to her. Suddenly, I felt very empty and closed in. And then she changed the subject. "Are you in college now, Tucker?"

"I've taken a year off," I lied. I don't know where this idea came from. I remember I was too ashamed to tell the truth. "I've been hitch-hiking around the country. I never know what the next day will bring. That's part of the excitement. I get jobs pumping gas, bagging groceries, waiting on tables, anything that will give me enough money to carry me to the next town. I'm sort of testing myself, and learning about the world."

"Oh, Tucker, how wonderful! How brave you are to take such chances! Aren't you afraid you'll run out of money and go hungry, or maybe run up against evil people?"

"Not really. Actually, the people I meet are pretty friendly and interesting. The down-and-out hitch hikers stick together like family, and there are a lot like me who are just adventurous."

"Where all have you been?" she asked, her big brown eyes full of wonder.

I was beginning to feel guilty about lying, but I kept it up, anyway. "I started out in June, right after Commencement. I peeled off my graduation gown, grabbed a bag I'd packed, and headed for the railroad yards. I rode freight cars south to the Carolinas, and then across Georgia and Alabama, all the way to the West Coast."

"Gee, I envy you! Boys are so lucky. A girl could never do anything like that."

The room suddenly got very warm, and I started to sweat from telling so many lies. So I changed the subject, before I got in too deep. "What's Bruce up to these days?"

"Oh, he's busy in school. He's on the honor roll and very active in sports. He can't make up his mind whether to go to medical school or to become quarterback for the Bears."

Diane and Bruce were very smart in school. She was encouraged to try out for *Quiz Kids*, a syndicated radio panel show, originating in Chicago. You had to be very smart and quick to be accepted. You had to be a genius.

"What about you? Did you ever try out for *Quiz Kids?"*

"No, it was flattering to be asked, but I was too shy. Anyway, I think my teachers overestimate me."

One of the things I liked about Diane was, she was very modest. You wouldn't know how smart she was, until you heard her recite in class or you looked at her report card. It's funny, but all the time growing up I hung out with the smart kids. I felt comfortable with them, even though I was dumb. And they felt comfortable with me. I often wonder why.

Just then I heard someone at the door. "That's Bruce!" Diane said and jumped up. "I didn't tell him you called last night. I wanted to surprise him."

The sight of Bruce coming into the room left me flabbergasted. He was no longer a scrawny little kid. At age fifteen, he was as tall as the door frame he stepped through. I shouldn't have been surprised, remembering how tall his father was.

"Bruce, do you know who this is?"

He took off his coat slowly, while looking down at me in silence, and after a moment said flatly, "Yeah, it's Tucker Amory."

"Bruce, shame on you! Tucker was your hero. Don't you remember?"

"Yeah, I guess so," he said, a little embarrassed.

"Tucker's become very worldly, Bruce. He hitch-hikes across the country, and rides freight trains, and lives by his wits. Isn't that exciting?"

"Uh, huh," was all he said, and looked like he didn't believe her.

"Bruce is going through what Mother calls his early adolescent rudeness period," Diane said, apologizing.

I got really depressed and angry. Angry at myself for lying to Diane. Angry at Bruce for his scorn and indifference. Angry at the world because so much had changed.

"Let's drive over to the old neighborhood," I said and jumped up. I had to find something that hadn't changed.

It didn't take long to get there. I parked across the street from Kregier Arms, the apartment hotel I'd called home back then and looked around in disbelief. I don't know what I expected, but nothing was the same. I guess you could say the building hadn't changed: red brick, leaded casement windows, and covering the walk the same blue awning with white piping along the scalloped edge, and heavy oak door, with deep panelling. But there were no kids in sight. And all the vacant lots were filled with new buildings—all glass and cold shiny metal that shamed the older buildings.

Where are Emil, and Billy, and Arnold? Where are the kids I played war with, and tag, and went to movies with? I had to turn my head, so Diane wouldn't see tears well up in my eyes. I glanced up at the bay window where I had spent so many hours looking out at the street below—across the vacant lots, across the sky where navy fighter planes flew practice missions. And I couldn't accept the fact that some other family lived there, and probably didn't even have any kids. And then I got angry at Dad for suggesting this trip.

Diane said she'd seen enough, but I couldn't leave yet; I had to find all the places that had given me happy memories. Parkside School looked the same. And the little corner grocery store where for a nickel I bought a package of Brach's chocolate covered mints on my way to school after lunch. There was a shortage of candy during the war, but the kindly old couple who ran the store kept a supply for me under the counter. I stopped the car and ran up, but there was nothing but emptiness behind a big dirty window. I drove past the Tivolli movie theater. It hadn't changed, its rows of blinking lights still drawing patrons into its magical world of make-believe. Next door, the familiar Chinese laundry still gave off a hot, damp smell of steam and starch, but there was a different Chinaman now. And there was Henry's, the steak house whose owner had his own cattle ranch out west, and all the steaks he served came from home grown beef.

"Why is this neighborhood so important to you, Tucker?"

I couldn't give her an answer right off. I've always been a very private person. I confide in no one. I wanted everyone to believe my life was normal, just like theirs—with a mother and father who lived together, and you could walk down the street together, holding hands, like a normal family, and share your thoughts.

"It's just that I had a lot of fun when I lived here, and you were my first sweetheart."

I drove Diane back to her parents' house, but before I said good-bye I put my arms around her and kissed her real hard.

"Do you remember the first time you tried to kiss me, and I wouldn't let you? I'm glad you didn't let that stop you this time." She said this so sweetly, my eyes began to water.

When I got back into the car and drove away, she waved from the living room window. We had parted with a promise to write and to see each other again.

"How was your day?" Dad asked.

"Okay, I found Diane, but everyone else has moved away." I didn't tell him how sad I felt.

In the car, on the way back home to Pennsylvania, the words of the song we'd sung at eighth grade graduation at Parkside School ran through my head: "When you walk through a storm keep your head up high, and don't be afraid of the dark." It seemed to me that the dark came down on me that day and soured all my sweet memories. And then I remembered the story about Paul that Willa Cather wrote. For the first time ever I began to fear for my future.

By the time we got back home to Grandmom's house, I had put Diane out of my mind, and Chicago, too. I knew I wouldn't write or see her again.

Dad never did say what he wanted to talk about "man to man." I learned later from Mom that it was her idea not his!

Seven

"Are you affirmative or negative?" Ned asked.

"I'm in favor of sending dollars to Britain."

"Why?"

"Because, egghead, we need a customer for our goods and an ally against communism," Tal said.

I was eavesdropping. Ned and Tal were seated in front of me at a weekly Sunday evening youth meeting in the basement of the First Presbyterian Church that Mom and I attended infrequently. I'd never been much of a churchgoer, and Mom didn't make me go, except on holidays like Christmas and Easter. But lately I started coming regularly because Ned Turner talked me into it. Ever since I made a big impression with the Armistice Day thing, he was after me, wanting to get to know me better, so I finally gave in. If it had been anyone else, I would've told him to shove it.

"The negative?" Ned asked.

"Britain's got to increase production and devalue its currency before America gives any more handouts."

"What are you guys talking about?" I asked.

"Upcoming debate. Britain was broke at the end of the war in 1945 and needed a lot of help from us," Tal said.

Ned Turner and Talbert Wishart were probably the smartest guys in this year's senior class. Their families were rich and very important in Coaltown society, Ned's father being head of Coaltown Steel, and Tal's father owner of a men's clothing store that stocked only expensive stuff. They were members of the country club, too.

Ned and I look alike. Everybody noticed this when he and his mom and dad moved to town a few years ago. His first appearance was at a summer dance at Lake Julia. When he walked in everybody stared at him, then turned and stared at me, and we both stared at each other, like we were long lost twins, or something. Height, weight, coloring, even our profiles are alike. It didn't take long for the jokes to start flowing about whose mom or dad had had an affair with the other guy's mom or dad. Looks is where it ends, though. In brains it's a different matter. He's smart and gets top grades.

Talbert Wishart is a husky, square-jawed ex football player. Ex because he tore up a knee in his sophomore year and had to quit—no longer top jock, but sure as hell top brain. Last year he won first prize in the state-wide American Legion Voice of Democracy Speech Contest. It got him a lunch at the governor's mansion and a four year college scholarship. This year he's president of Sock and Buskin and the senior class, and important in a whole lot of other stuff.

Tal and Ned were good buddies. They talked a lot about things in the daily news, like Britain's post-war economy and the big threat of a nation-wide labor strike in the steel industry. I couldn't get interested in stuff like this. I tried, but I soon got bored. The only front page story that got my attention was President Truman's telling everybody that Russia had the bomb. Mom read the society page—gossipy stories about people she didn't even know. There were even stories about people having birthday parties, but my birthdays never got into the city newspaper. The back pages were full of ads for groceries, cars, and kitchen stuff. One day an ad did make me sit up and take notice—the grand opening of the Park Burlesque Theater. Strippers Princess Taranova and Betty Young the Lady Godiva were the attractions. Minors were not allowed, of course, but some of us guys were going to try, including Ned and Tal. We figured if we dressed up in Sunday clothes and wore felt hats we'd get in.

The meeting came to order and Alistair McNab, the new assistant preacher, led off with the Lord's Prayer. McNab had been a chaplain in the Navy. Tonight he was wearing his officer's blue coat, minus gold braid; the brass buttons had been replaced with plain ones. He wasn't very popular because he smiled all the time about everything and nothing. Anybody who smiles all the time at nothing has got to be a phony.

"Before we start the meeting," McNab said, "I want to announce the committee chairmen for the midnight New Year's Eve party." This annual bash was supposed to keep the congregation's teens off the streets and out of the bars and nightclubs in Coaltown. It seemed to work, but the party didn't stop anyone from boozing. Stuff got smuggled in, and both guys and girls got drunk, and expelled, and parents had to come and carry home their boozed-up little darlings.

McNab named committees for refreshments, decorations, tickets, chaperones, dance band, and entertainment. He put Ned and Tal on entertainment and then said, "Chairman of this committee is Tucker Amory."

At first, I didn't believe what I'd heard, but when it sank in my first thought was, how do I get out of this? Before I could protest, McNab said, "Julie Rankin is our discussion leader tonight. Julie, are you ready?"

Her topic was teen drinking and alcoholism. She handed out a dittoed questionnaire. The questions were supposed to help a teen tell whether he or she was a real boozer. The timeliness of the topic had to do with the upcoming holidays, she said.

I knew lots of teens who drank, mostly the rich, who could afford it, and many of the smart teens like Ned and Tal—them in particular. But booze was not a problem for me. I never touched the stuff, partly because of what I had seen it do to Dad, and partly because it smelled so bad.

All through the meeting I tried to think of a way to escape being chairman. I mean I was really in a panic! "I haven't any experience!" I whispered to Ned. He ignored me. "How about you, Tal? You know a lot about this kind of thing!"

"Sorry, pal, my family's spending Christmas in Hawaii. I'll be back in time for the party, but I won't be around for rehearsals."

"Can I count on you to entertain?" Already I was beginning to sound like I was going to do it!

"Relax, Tucker, I'll be there. Just give me time to work something up."

Tal's assurance wasn't enough to calm my anxiety. I looked around the room, but couldn't settle on anyone I was close with, to dump the job McNab had dumped on me.

Julie droned on about the evils of booze, but I didn't pay attention. Finally, she finished her presentation and then invited everyone to sample the drinks she had setup: "mocktails" she called them. They looked alcoholic, because they had the right color and were served in fancy glasses, but contained only fruit juice and olives or cherries. Ned slipped a flask from his back pocket and splashed something into his and Tal's glasses.

"Talbert's the one who suggested you for chairman. You'll have to do it; everyone else has been given an assignment," McNab said, when I tried to corner him and beg off. "Ned'll give you lots of help," he said, and turned away. So I was stuck with it. Any time a teacher laid something like this on me, I just ignored it. But something kept me from ignoring it this time, and it made me angry with myself, to think I was actually going to do it.

Several days went by, and I hadn't come up with a single idea. In school Tal asked how it was shaping up, and I just shrugged, trying to act cool. He gave me a worried look and told me I'd better get on the ball, before it was too late.

When I got home that night, Mom noticed there was something wrong, which surprised me because I was always pretty good about hiding my feelings from her, and reluctant to ask for advice, because I always got a lecture about being irresponsible.

"Why didn't you tell me earlier?" she said. I'd not considered that she'd done a lot of amateur theatricals when she was young. Right off she gave me lots of good ideas. "Ned's an amateur magician; he performed at a DAR luncheon once. There are soloists in the church choir you could ask to perform. Has a dance band been hired yet? Every band has solo instrumentalists who love to show their best. And what about Talbert Wishart? He did a very funny monologue once at a Woman's Club luncheon."

"What's a monologue?"

"A little play with only one performer. Ask him to do comedy. Jerry Barber who goes to our church sings baritone in a quartet. Maybe he'd talk the other three into singing at the party with him." Mom's ideas came at me faster than I could write them down. "And why don't *you* do something, too? Act out the pantomimes. The ones I've seen you do in front of the mirror in Grandmom's bedroom." This kind of caught me by surprise. I didn't know she'd seen me doing Charlie Chaplin and Red Skelton imitations. I must have forgotten to close the door sometimes. She was right; from spending all those weekends at the movies, I had a pretty good collection of imitations.

"What do you think?" I said to Ned the next day.

"Sounds good to me, but everyone's seen my magic act. I'll do it if I can work up a few new tricks."

I stopped Tal just as he was coming out of physics, but I couldn't remember the word Mom used. "It's a solo—a speech of some kind."

"You don't mean a soliloquy, do you?"

"Mom said it's a guy playing a role by himself."

"Monologue is what she meant. I'll see what I can find, but it's not going to be easy entertaining a bunch of rowdies at a midnight dance. A couple of days later Tal said he'd found a comic monologue by Anton Chekhov called "On the Harmfulness of Tobacco." Chekhov, he said, was a Russian writer.

"What's so funny about it?" I asked, more than a little doubtful.

"The speaker's a boring little jerk. He's been asked to deliver a lecture against smoking. His audience is all just plain folks, and he bores the hell out of them. Before he gets very far into it, he loses his train of thought and lapses into a long, windy complaint about how he's henpecked at home, and how his daughters manipulate him. The farther he gets off his subject the funnier it gets. At the end, he breaks down and loses complete control of himself, even forgetting he's talking to an audience."

It didn't sound very funny to me, but I knew I could trust Tal, everybody else did.

During the week between Christmas and New Year's, I held rehearsals. McNab had named a replacement for Tal on the committee, but I found I didn't need much help, just someone to do a few technical things, like set up a platform and a microphone in the gym. Ned rehearsed his magic act, with a few new tricks; a couple of soloists from the church choir each sang a popular ballad; and I did Red Skelton's imitation of a fat lady getting out of bed in the morning and putting on her clothes; and a little scene where Charlie Chaplin's little tramp tries to save a poor street girl from a guy who's beating her, not knowing she's a prostitute. Altogether, I figured I had an hour-long floor show. When the rehearsal ended, I strolled home feeling very satisfied with myself. Big white flakes of new snow floated down and covered the old. All around me Christmas lights winked in the windows of homes and shops. Little kids on brand new sleds rode merrily down backyard slopes. It was the happiest holiday season I'd ever had. But when everything seems to be going just right, something always seems to spoil it, right? When I got to Grandmom's house, Dad was there. He'd gone back to Columbus after Christmas Day, so I hadn't expected to see him again until Easter. But there was the coral pink Kaiser, and him sitting in the big chair just inside the front door.

As usual, he didn't give a reason for coming. We ate supper. Everyone talked about stuff that didn't interest me, until the subject of New Year's Eve came up and Dad was told about the all-night party.

"You're telling me he's going to stay out all night! He's only eighteen! I suppose he's taking a girl to this party! You know what that could lead to! Where is this party, anyway? At someone's house—a nightclub?" With eyes blazing he turned to me, and ordered me to cancel my date and stay at home.

Stunned by the heat of his anger, Mom and I just stared at each other in disbelief. Then she spoke up and explained all about the party and my role as entertainment chairman and performer, and that I certainly could not cancel a date at the last minute. By the time she got to the end of her explanation, her voice had risen to equal his in anger. Dad then answered back, with more anger. "I don't care what you say, I'm his father and I'll decide what's best!"

I pushed back my chair and stomped out of the dining room. Nothing was going to keep me from going to the party, least of all someone who was no longer big enough to stop me. I ran into the bedroom, grabbed my rented tux and dashed out the front door. I drove around for a while in Grandmom's car, trying to decide where to go for the remaining few hours before the party. I decided on the church. When I got there the janitor was the only one in sight, so I didn't have to explain myself to anybody.

In my hurry I had forgotten my date's corsage back home in the fridge. For a while I poked around among the crepe paper decorations in the gym, hoping an hour or so would be enough to take the steam out of the shouting match, and then called Mom.

"Tucker, it's all right now. I'll have the corsage at the front door, so you won't have to face him."

When the time came, I dressed in the gym locker room. During the days leading up to New Year's Eve, I'd almost forgotten to rent a tux and was so late the rental store had few to pick from. I had to settle for a 1920s style coat, single-breasted, and a vest. Nobody wore a vest with a tux, anymore. But when I put it all on, I liked the look of it: starched white formal dress shirt with detachable wing collar (nobody wore wing collars anymore), jeweled studs, and shiny black shoes. I felt like a movie star, like I was Fred Astaire and Ginger Rogers was my date. Comb in hand I worked to get my hair just right. Most of the guys in school wore duck-tail cuts. You know, where on top you have a crew cut, but you let your hair grow long on the sides, then comb in greasy stuff and sweep it back into what looks like a duck's ass. Not me. I hated that look. I parted my hair in the regular way, combed it straight back on top and then pushed it forward into a wave, using a little water on the comb.

I tap-danced into the empty gym. The thought flashed across my mind for a minute that I looked like Paul in the story by Willa Cather, and it gave me a little chill. I stepped onto the platform the committee had placed there for the band and the floor show. I pulled the microphone up to me and tried out my welcoming speech. "Good evening out there. Welcome to the fifth annual First Presbyterian Church New Year's Eve party. Here's Mat Medley and the Rhythmaires! Everybody get up and dance! Hit it, Mat!" This is what I had settled on, after trying out several openers, all of which sounded pretty dumb.

Just then McNab popped in, to check up on things, and he wasn't very happy. It wasn't the streamer ceiling strung high up across the gym from one side of the spectator gallery to the other that bothered him, it was the streamer curtain that dropped from the gallery and hid the guests' tables from the eyes of the chaperones. But it was too late to make changes, so all he did was grumble a little.

My date was Charity Knox. Her father was senior minister of the church. She was a year older than me, and considering I was a year older than just about everybody at the party, Charity's age practically put her in a different league. She was tall and stately. In high heels she would have been a fraction of an inch taller than me. Her hair was long, dark and glossy. She wore expensive big city clothes. I had asked her to be my date, as a favor to Rev. Knox. She was kind of legendary in Coaltown. Like many preachers' and teachers' kids, she was very rebellious. There was a story about her having to go away and finish school while living with her aunt. When she returned to Coaltown a year later, she just stayed at home, didn't hold a job or do much of anything, except a little volunteer work. She was a heavy smoker. She always sat alone at Sunday night youth group meetings and looked bored, and though some of the guys spoke to her, the girls shied away. It was one of those situations where everybody knows the story, but no one ever mentions it, probably because everyone liked her father and didn't want to create unnecessary embarrassment. There had been lots of hints from her father to the guys about how he'd like it for somebody to ask Charity to the party. I hadn't been dating anyone at the time, so I took took the hint.

Before she said yes, she took a deep drag on her cigarette, sort of sizing me up, probably wondering why I wanted to date her. I could have told her that my reputation wasn't so great, either. "Sure," she said, and let out a long plume of smoke. When I called for Charity at her parents' house, she really looked pretty in her white evening gown. It was a tight fit and she had the right figure for it. And she seemed really happy she'd been asked.

When we arrived at the gym, the Rhythmaires were setting up, each with a music stand bearing Mat Medley's initials scrolled in glittering letters. I searched for the entertainers, Tal, in particular, since I hadn't seen him all week. He and Ned had arrived together, with their dates, and it was pretty obvious they'd been drinking.

I stepped up to microphone and welcomed everyone. The first dance number was the theme song of Vaughn Monroe's orchestra, "Racing With the Moon." I took Charity's hand, led her unto the floor, put my arm around her waist, gave a sigh of relief, and danced. Everyone gave us the eye, Charity's tight gown and all.

Two minutes till midnight, Mat started the countdown. Noisemakers shrieked in the excited air, and when the big moment came, he pulled a rope, uncovering a sign that read "1950" in big gold letters. All around us couples kissed and toasted the new year with punch, which someone had secretly laced with gin. The church kitchen was set up for a midnight buffet supper, and everyone lined up with paper plates and plastic dinnerware.

"Are you nervous, Tucker?" Charity asked. She could see that I wasn't eating. The floor show was up next, and I would soon have to do my pantomimes.

Ned Turner was master of ceremonies. He bounced onto the stage, grabbed the microphone, swung it around full circle, like they do in a real nightclub, told a few jokes, ending with his favorite: "Hello, there, all you love-starved teenagers! You know what a teenager is? (pause) Hormones with feet!" His timing was perfect. He waited for the laughter to die down, and then introduced the first act: Sally Miles singing "It's Only a Paper Moon." Ned followed this with his magic act. He pulled playing cards out of nowhere, made a rabbit mysteriously appear and disappear, turned a cane into a string of silk handkerchiefs, and called up a volunteer in the audience to assist with a few card tricks. His tricks were old, but he was really clever with his hands, so he got a big hand from the audience. Next was Barb Arbour. Mocking little Shirley Temple's cutsey delivery, she sang "Mares Eat Oats and Does Eat Oats and Little Lambs Eat Ivy", which brought a few laughs. Then Sally and Barb sang in harmony, "Rum and Coca Cola." Then it was my turn.

Ned introduced me and said I had just finished a sensational week of performances at the Park Burlesque, which brought more boos that laughs.

I waddled out in my Charlie Chaplin makeup and costume, twirling a bamboo cane and did all the familiar turns and twitches Chaplin made famous in silent films. Because I didn't have to speak lines, I wasn't at all nervous. Charity played the girl. The little tramp in this scene doesn't know the poorly dressed girl he's trying to rescue from a beating is really a prostitute in the clutches of her pimp, played by Tal. She won't accept the little tramp's help and even begins to beat him up. Charity pretended to knock me around the stage a little, and then the scene ended with me lying on the floor, looking bewildered, and the prostitute and her pimp strolling away arm in arm. When I picked myself up and waddled off, I heard lots of cheers and applause.

Ned and Tal were waiting for me offstage. "My god, Amory, where have you been all these years?" Ned exclaimed.

"That was great! You had them eating out of your hands!" said Tal.

"That was the best Chaplin imitation I've ever seen!" Ned said.

Charity, too, was excited. But her father, who watched from backstage, turned away. And then it dawned on me—the role I had asked her to play! When she accepted it, she hadn't given any indication that someone might make something of it.

While Tal did his monologue for the audience, I changed for my next act, the Red Skelton imitation. The costume this time was all make-believe, showing only in gestures. When my time came, the lights were turned out momentarily, and then a spotlight caught me lying across the seat of a straight-back chair, arms and legs outstretched. I reached out and turned off an imaginary alarm clock, stretched, yawned, and rose from the chair, making exaggerated gestures. After pretending to wiggle out of a slinky nightgown, I slipped my arms into an imaginary bra, struggling mightily to fasten it in back. Next, I wiggled and tugged at an invisible girdle, all the while struggling for breath, and, when that was finally accomplished, slid invisible nylon hose up my legs, snagging them on a toe nail. I then pretended to slide a dress over my head, snagging it on a hairpin. When all was complete, I waddled off in such a way as to suggest that everything fit so tightly I could hardly move or breathe. Each comic gesture drew shrieks of laughter from the girls and whistles from the guys. When it was over, Ned and Tal poured out more praise. A chant went up from the audience, "Tucker! Tucker! Tucker!"

"They want more!" Charity said, and she pushed me out on stage.

I grabbed my bamboo cane, did a few Chaplin-like turns and falls, and waddled off. The applause kept up, and I was called back to take several more bows.

After the floor show, the evening settled down to dreamy music and slow dancing. Charity and I danced cheek to cheek and caught lots of glances from the couples all around us. I couldn't make out the reason for so much attention. Was it Charity or me—her reputation or my performance? Maybe it was both.

Eight

"Well, I'm very proud of you," Mom said. "Rev. McNab called to tell me the entertainment was very appropriate, that the floor show was very well-organized, and you were a big hit." Mom spoke between clenched teeth because her mouth was full of straight pins she was using to lay out a dress pattern on the dining room table.

Word about my big success got around in school. Even some of my teachers heard about it. Señorita Witherspoon said she wasn't surprised at all, considering how well I'd done the Armistice Day thing.

Feralman stopped me in the hall. By the look on his face, I thought I'd done something wrong, again. "Well, well, Tucker," he said, looking down his nose, "I hear you had 'em all laughing on New Year's Eve." He said it like I'd done something stupid and embarrassed myself.

A smart-ass girl in English class asked, giggling, "Who taught you how a woman dresses, Tucker?" I told her I picked it up at the Park Burlesque.

Tal talked me into joining Sock and Buskin, saying he had a role for me in a one-act he was directing. And he insisted I sign up for Miss Marlowe's second semester theater class.

Suddenly, I was getting a lot of attention from people who had always ignored me. I wasn't used to it, and I resented it a little, because it laid a lot on me. I used to know who I was—a dumb guy who couldn't do anything right. My irresponsibility had given me freedom, and nobody bothered with me. I didn't have to do homework because nobody expected it. I didn't have to take on important tasks because nobody trusted me. I was free! Now, all of a sudden, I wasn't so sure about myself, and it scared me. I couldn't even run away, like the time I ran from Bill Spondike. I didn't exactly put it into words at the time, like now. Things were happening so fast, I didn't even have time to think about it.

Sock and Buskin met once a month in the auditorium. There was usually a guest speaker, and sometimes a kid who had been to New York would report on a Broadway play he'd seen. At the January meeting, the first I attended, we were assigned tasks in stage makeup. Miss Marlowe gave us a few basic principles and then told us to be creative and make ourselves up as a character in a play. I didn't know any characters, but I was curious to see what I'd look like as a very old man with a beard. I covered my head with a wild-looking wig and carefully combed out the woolly beard stuff. Not knowing the adhesive, called spirit gum, was strong—it smelled like ether—and stung, as I painted it all over my face—I had everyone in the room gasping for air! "Just a little dab, Tucker! That's all it takes!" said Miss Marlowe, covering her nose with the back of her hand. But it was too late. Tal said I looked like a drunken Santa Claus. Ned chimed in with "Moses! That's who he is."

"That's a very good King Lear," Miss Marlowe said. I didn't know who King Lear was, but I agreed with her, anyway. "For those of you who don't know, in the play Lear is an aged king who abdicates, gives away his kingdom to two mean-spirited, ungrateful daughters. He banishes a third daughter from the kingdom, the one who is loyal and loving and true. And he lives to regret his mistake. Every major character suffers a terrible fate. Lear goes mad, his lovely third daughter Cordelia dies, and the Duke of Gloucester is brutally blinded by one of the villains. Shakespeare wrote it during a dark time in his life." And then she added, "Isn't that right, Tucker? Not many of my students select a Shakespearean character for practice in stage makeup," and she gave me a knowing wink. I tried to smile, but the spirit gum, stiff and dry on my cheeks, held the woolly stuff as tight as a muzzle.

At the end of January, when second semester started, I signed up for theater class, and found myself among the smartest upperclassmen at Cruhl High, which made me feel kind of strange but also a little proud. Miss Marlowe gave me a leading role in a one-act called *The Reform of Sterling Silverhead.* It was a farce; the characters had names like Dupe Darkly and Mama Ghoul. I played Sterling, a comic good guy who dates the daughter of the bad family, the Ghouls. The Ghoul family tries to reform Sterling, which means they try to turn him into a bad guy. The play had lots of funny lines and silly situations, and I enjoyed doing it. And I learned a fancy new term: *double entendre.*

"What's this, Mom?" At the supper table one night, she placed a newspaper item beside my plate.

"It's from today's *Times.* The Williamstown Playhouse is holding tryouts," she said, as she passed the potatoes.

It was a short item, just a notice saying that teenage boys were needed for an upcoming production of *The Corn Is*

Green, a play about poor, illiterate kids who lived in the coal fields of Wales, and a teacher who opens a school.

"Hand me the butter, please. Well, would you like to audition? It's Sunday afternoon."

"Yeah, I see that. But suppose they give me a part. I'd have to go to Williamstown for rehearsals. I'd have to take Grandmom's car."

"It might be fun to try out, even if you don't get a part."

The Williamstown Playhouse was a semi-professional theater company. Actors were local amateurs, but the director and scene designer were hired pros. They did six shows a year. Each show ran nightly for two weeks, sixteen performances in all, two of which were matinees. Rehearsals would be daily, which would mean I'd be hogging Grandmom's car every day. The reality of it didn't make me very hopeful, but what the heck, trying out would be fun, as Mom said.

When Sunday came, Mom tagged along. Williamstown was a big city fifteen miles from Coaltown. We knew it pretty well because of its large downtown shopping area and popular movie houses. We found the theater, a converted movie house, on the main street. A sign pointed the way to the stage door down an alley. Inside we found ourselves backstage. There were flats, ropes and pulleys and spotlights everywhere. The air smelled of grease paint, dust, fresh lumber, and stage paint. The stage was set up like a rich man's drawing room, with flats painted to look like wood paneling. I learned later it was a setup for Noel Coward's *Private Lives*.

Mom and I introduced ourselves to a woman carrying a clipboard, who seemed to be in charge. She told us to take a seat in the front of the house, and that I should wait to be called. A lone work light cast a dim glow across the stage and made the drawing room set dull and lifeless. But I knew that the right lighting, flowing down from a bank of gelatins hidden in the loft, would bring it all to life, and I felt a tingle of excitement.

About a dozen teens like me were seated around us. They seemed very much at home here, like they'd tried out often and had probably been picked before for plays.

At two o'clock sharp the woman who greeted us walked on stage, her high heels clicking loudly across the bare boards. "Welcome to the Williamstown Playhouse. We thank you for giving up your Sunday afternoon for us. Each of you will be asked to come up and read a scene with a member of the cast. André Swan is seated behind you. He will listen to you read and talk with you after. If this is your first time, please fill out an audition card before you leave."

She walked off and threw a switch. The stage suddenly flooded with light. A man's voice behind us called for the first person to go forward. Each was asked to give his name and age and to take a seat beside a male member of the cast. Every guy who read before me seemed to know the director, André Swan, who was seated behind us. Some even addressed him by his first name. They all read their lines like they already knew the play, and some even knew some lines by heart. They had strong voices and acted well. God, I thought, what chance have I got against all these bright, experienced guys! When my turn came, all the nervousness I brought with me disappeared, because I knew I didn't stand a chance. So I took my good old time getting up on stage and just sort of dropped limply onto the chair.

"Hi, I'm Hamilton Pridwell—Morgan Evans in the play," he said, like I knew what he was talking about. He was about my height, but a couple of years older than me, very friendly, and I felt at ease. He handed me a script.

"You haven't told me your name, young man!" said a stern voice, beyond the lights.

"Sorry, sir. Tucker Amory. I'm a senior at Cruhl High School." I told him I was eighteen, which was not true because I'd had a birthday a few days before.

"Where in God's name is that?"

"What?"

"That high school! I've never heard of it!"

"In Coaltown," I said.

"We're wasting time! Get on with it!"

This guy's impatience, and my discouragement, soured me to this whole experience, and I didn't care how I came off. So I slumped down in my seat, hung my ass on the edge of the chair, stretched my legs out, crossed my ankles, and holding the script loosely, mumbled my lines. I didn't even care about being insolent.

When I finished reading and looked up, some old guy was standing up close and staring at me. Very long gray hair, glasses, a scarf tied around his neck and tucked into the open front of his shirt.

"How much experience have you had?"

"None," I said, just as abruptly as he'd spoken to me.

He studied me very closely for a moment and then said to his assistant, "Good, I want him for Robbart Robbatch." He turned away as abruptly as he spoke and signaled for the next candidate to come forward.

"Congratulations, Tucker!" It was the assistant. She introduced herself as Joan Griffin and put a script in my hand, and told me that rehearsals would begin the following week, at the home of the woman playing the leading role, and not at the theater because the stage was still set for the current production.

I was so shocked, I hardly heard her words. "Can you be there at seven o'clock in the evening a week from Monday? The address is 795 Fifth Avenue.

"He'll be *there*," Mom answered.

"You do understand he'll have to be available for rehearsals quite often during the next six weeks and almost daily the closer we get to opening night?" As she turned to leave, she added, "By the way, Tucker, your pretending arrogance and insolence was very convincing. You must know the play."

"*Yes*," Mom said.

I was still in a daze, and all this went so fast I couldn't keep up. Mom's easy acceptance of it all was as surprising to me as my winning a role in the play.

In the car on the way back to Coaltown I finally had a chance to sort things out. "Mom, what do you think? All those guys who did so well, and he picked me!"

"Well, Tucker, maybe they didn't have what André Swan was looking for, and you did."

"Maybe he liked the way I paired up with the guy who's playing the male lead. That sometimes makes a difference," I said, but Mom didn't answer me.

At home I made myself comfortable on the living room sofa and read the play. It was about a teacher who sets up a school for children of all ages in a Welsh village. The children have had no formal education because they have to work long hours in the coal mines—even the littlest kids! The oldest among them are insolent and unruly. I was to play Robbart Robbatch, best friend of the male lead Morgan Evans, so I thought I had a big part. Morgan and Robbart make their first appearance in the second scene of the first act. The stage directions said, "Five black-faced miners, between twelve and sixteen years of age, wearing caps, mufflers, boots and corduroys embedded in coal dust swagger onto the stage acting very sassy and impudent. Each face, indistinguishable from the others." Robbart's first line is, "Be mai'n ddeud?" I read through to the end of the first scene. Great, I said to myself, not only will no one in the audience recognize me under the black coal dust, no one will understand a word I say—all my lines are in Welsh!

"Nawn—(Rises) i drio malchi—dewch(All rise—start off) mae'n well nag eistedd yma—dewch..." How would I ever learn to pronounce such strange-looking words? Reading to the end, I discovered Robbart appears in only two scenes!

Over the clatter of Mom's sewing machine I shouted, "Why should I spend a lot of time traveling to Williamstown, wearing out Grandmom's old car, just to act in two scenes, wearing a dirty face and speaking lines no one will understand? In the second scene, I don't even have any *lines*!"

Mom moved her foot and the clattering stopped. "Hm," she said. "I agree, Tucker, it doesn't sound like much of a part, for the time you'd be putting into it." She thought a minute, and then said, "There's a lot you'd learn while waiting to do your scenes; André Swan is a professional, don't forget. And not having any lines to speak in your second scene doesn't mean you wouldn't have to act."

Mom was right about that. Even though I didn't speak in my second scene, a classroom full of unruly students, with me as one of them, there was plenty of opportunity for me to improvise pantomimes, which everyone said I did so well.

I described the audition to Miss Marlowe, next day in school. "I'm not sure why you were chosen for the role, Tucker, but I can tell you what Miss Witherspoon and I noticed, when you spoke at the Armistice Day assembly: you have what is called stage presence, or empathy— when you appeared on stage, the audience watched and listened. It's an indescribable quality, and it's something one is born with."

That was a whole lot for me to swallow all at once, but I sure was grateful she said it.

Fifth Avenue in Williamstown is where the rich live. It's a main street and easy to find. The number I was given,

795, turned out to be a huge red brick mansion set about a hundred yards back from the road. There was even a gate and a gate house at the head of the drive. It was the home of Helen Meyer, the woman who was playing Miss Moffat, the school teacher, the leading role in the play. (I learned later that her husband's money paid the salaries of the pros—the hired director and the scene designer—in exchange for which she was given a leading role in a play of her own choice each season.)

A uniformed butler opened the front door and led me into the hall. The rehearsal was held in the library, a big wood-paneled, book-filled room. The furnishings were pretty rich, with oriental rugs and heavy tables and chairs. Upholstered pieces seemed to swallow the people sitting on them. André Swan, frowning, was sprawled on a huge wing-back chair covered in a tapestry-like fabric.

"We'll start with the boys' scene in Act I. Morgan and Robbart on one end of the bench, three young miners the other end. Take your places, please. Begin."

I'd brought a miner's flat cap with me. I set it on my head at a rakish angle, put my hands on my hips, spread my legs out in front, thrust out my chin, curled my lips into an impudent grin and acted real cocky, saying the Welsh words as best I could, which was okay because we were told someone would teach us later the correct pronunciation. The director stopped the rehearsal many times to give directions. But he never corrected me. I could tell he liked what I did.

During a break, Hamilton Pridwell, who played Morgan Evans, as I said before, pulled me aside. "Everybody calls me Ham," he said. "I suppose it's a good nickname for an actor, and some say it fits me!" he joked. He asked me about myself and seemed genuinely interested in my answers. I told him everything about how I got interested in acting, but I didn't tell him anything about my school life or my family. We talked a lot between scenes, and we got along pretty well, and as the weeks and months went by, we became close friends.

"It's okay to address the director by his first name," Ham said, "everybody does."

Nine

Ham was only two years older than me, but he had already graduated from Yale. English had been his major, and he planned to be a writer. He was doing *The Corn Is Green* just to get some acting experience and learn how to write dialogue.

"Experimenting right now, Robbatch, dabbling in acting and doing a little writing," he said. "Maybe I'll pursue a master's in writing, or just hole up in a garret or a cold water flat and teach myself."

"Garret? Cold water flat?"

"Attic on the Left Bank. Apartment in the Village."

I had no idea what he meant, and I didn't ask because sometimes, if he thought I'd asked a stupid question, he ignored it.

Ham's family lived in Helen Meyer's neighborhood, in an English Tudor house. I'd learned that much about houses in theater class. His parents' house looked a little like Shakespeare's birthplace I'd seen in a photo, but much bigger. His bedroom was as big as the whole first floor of Grandmom's house. Big, heavy, dark furniture with richly grained wood and heavy brass drawer pulls, a desk my dad would've envied, two tall dressers, one for winter and one for summer clothes, a high four-poster bed with posts as big as soccer balls. He even had a sofa, with thick rich upholstery. A walk-in closet held a long rack of suits and tweed jackets. Hanging on the walls were a tennis racquet, cricket bat, crossed polo mallets, and photos of himself posed with prep school teams and Yale clubs. Like André Swan he had a casual English elegance. I felt uncomfortable the first time I saw all he had, but, as I said before, he was friendly, and I was flattered by the interest he took in me, and I soon got used to the rich stuff that surrounded him. I even got to the point I wasn't afraid to show my ignorance.

"Robbatch, you've been stuck in Coaltown too long," he'd say, when I said something dumb, or, "I don't believe you were born in Brooklyn and grew up in New York and Chicago. The village hick you pretend to be is just an act, right?"

His parents didn't seem to know what to make of me. When he introduced me, they studied me carefully and every time I visited always seemed to be watching me.

Ham was the first person I ever confided in, partly because he was easy to be with, and partly because he kept asking me about myself. "Why do you want to know so much about me?"

"I'm a writer, Robbatch, I'll probably put you in a book some day."

I didn't believe that, but I told him what he wanted to know. "You say Coaltown's only fifteen miles from here. Never been there. No reason to go. Tell me about it, your family, too," he said, one Saturday after a rehearsal. We were in his bedroom, him stretched out on the bed, me swallowed up in the sofa.

"It's a long boring story, I can't believe you really want to hear it."

"So what else have we got on today?"

"Okay, but stay awake, it gets a little complicated, especially the part about my parents' separations."

Ham snapped his fingers, imitating André, when he ordered a scene to begin, and said, "Action."

"Mom and Dad were born in Coaltown, but I was born in Brooklyn, Dad having taken a job there after they were married."

"Job?"

"Salesman for a company that contracted window glass and aluminum fascia for Manhattan's new skyscrapers. Dad won the contract for the glass and aluminum plates you see today on the face of the Empire State Building. That was about twenty years ago, but he can still tell you the number of windows it has. On the day it was announced he won the contract, he celebrated by buying himself a black Chesterfield overcoat with velvet collar and a black bowler hat. Mom said he looked as handsome as Edward, Prince of Wales."

"Hm."

"Soon after, we moved to Jackson Heights. That's where I went to first grade. But because of the Depression Dad lost his job, he and Mom separated, and she and I moved in with Grandmom in Coaltown. That's where I went second through fifth grade. In 1941 Mom and Dad got back together and we moved to Chicago and lived there till the end of the war. Then they separated again, and Mom and I moved back to Coaltown, where I started freshman year in the fall of '45. So, here I am. End of story."

"Was it the Depression or marital problems?"

"If you're asking about the separations, I'd have to say both."

"Four or five years, and then back together? Hm. I know parents who've separated, but I've never heard of any like yours. Most either divorce or reconcile. Period." Ham lay staring at the ceiling for a minute, thinking. "Somewhere there's a year missing. You told me you were born in '31, in January. This is February 1950, so you're nineteen, right?"

"True. I love high school so much I'm repeating my senior year. Gotta make sure I do it right, before I step out into the cold, cruel world." Ham's whimsy had begun to rub off on me. "The truth is—I flunked." I couldn't have confessed this so easily to anyone else, but his devil-may-care spirit had affected me.

"That must have taken guts. I don't think I could have pulled it off."

"Yep, repeating my senior year is my great experiment in education."

Did he believe my story, or was he quick to sense the shame I was covering up? Changing the subject, he asked, "What do you read?"

"Drama and poetry, mostly. Eugene O'Neill and the modern poets: Robinson, Frost, Masters, Sandburg."

"Rubbish, Robbatch. O'Neill is a good choice, but your poets are second rate. You should read T.S. Eliot, Ezra Pound, and the French symbolists. No novelists? Oscar Wilde? Truman Capote? Gore Vidal? I'll lend you my copy of *Other Voices, Other Rooms.*"

I told him I'd read *Of Human Bondage* by Somerset Maugham, a story I could identify with, being that the main character's a loser, but he didn't comment on that.

"Tell me about Coaltown. How far from Pittsburgh?"

"About seventy-five miles, a nowhere town of twenty thousand. They make steel, electrical transformers, railroad tank cars, metal tubing and stuff."

"Stuff? That's not a very good Chamber of Commerce word, Robbatch."

"It's smoky because of the mills. Mom says at night when the fires from the blast furnaces light up the sky she thinks of the scene in *Gone With the Wind* when Sherman burned Atlanta."

"Hm."

"My mother's family owns one of the factories. Maybe you've heard of it: Reimer Manufacturing Company. They make gas furnaces.

"This house is heated by a Reimer."

"If you think we're rich, you're wrong. We live in a small, two-story white frame house in a working-class neighborhood. Grandmom gets her income from dividends the factory pays her, but it's not much, and money paid by the married couple who rent the upstairs."

"Where's your dad?"

"He lives in Columbus and sells commercial refrigeration."

"Go on."

"Grandmom's house is so small I don't have my own bedroom. I sleep on a roll-away in the dining room. When I was little, I slept on the sofa in the living room. I was always embarrassed when my playmates came to the house. There was no room to play, and I didn't want them to see where I slept."

"Let's see if I have this right. You and your mother live on your grandmother's income because you get no support from your father."

"Right." It was painful, hearing someone say it like that.

"Tell me about your mother and grandmother."

"Mom's very pretty. She was a dancer when she was young, and a local celebrity. Her friends tell me that, so I guess it's true."

"That's where you get your looks and talent, Robbatch."

"Granddad was going to take her to New York and enroll her in a big-time dance school, but he died suddenly, and that ended it."

"So what did she do?"

"Nothing. Worked for a while as a retail clerk, that's all."

"I don't get it. If your mother's family owns Reimer, why do your mother and grandmother live so poorly? Why didn't your mother go to college?"

"Grandmom didn't get along with her inlaws, after Granddad died. They didn't offer any help, and she was too proud to ask. The only Reimer Mom's close with is one of her brothers. Many of the Reimers barely know about us."

"My family quarrels, too."

"Grandmom's very quiet and reserved. She doesn't talk to me about much, unlike most grandmothers, who smother kids with love. She never hugs or kisses me, but that's okay, I guess."

"Victorian. Does your mother still clerk?"

"No. She spends most of her time at her sewing machine. Mom seems to think she has to keep up appearances, and maintain her idea of status—the grand life she lived before Granddad died. So she makes the clothes she sees in the fashion magazines, a whole wardrobe each new year."

"And your dad?"

"Very bright. Speed reader. Total recall. Whiz in math and science. Never had to study hard to learn in school, and got top grades in every subject. He also happens to be tone deaf and color blind!"

"I hear anger in those words, and bitterness. You don't get along, do you?"

"I'm not as smart as him. I didn't inherit his brains. But everybody thinks I should be smart, just like him. I don't even look like him, though some people think they see a resemblance. He's blonde and blue-eyed. I get my brown hair and brown eyes from the Reimers."

"Guys, it seems, often take from their mother's side."

"The best time I ever had with dad was when I was nine years old, and it was the Fourth of July. But it didn't start out to be a best time. What happened was, all the kids in the neighborhood had caps for their toy pistols, and firecrackers. But Mom wouldn't let me have anything. All day I kept asking for money to buy what every other kid had, but all she said was no. But late in the afternoon Dad made a surprise visit."

"This was in Coaltown?"

"He opened the trunk of his car, and there was this huge box of fireworks. The news spread, and the whole neighborhood gathered at Grandmom's house. There were caps for pistols, firecrackers, cherry bombs that exploded like cannons, sparklers, and skyrockets that filled the night sky with wonderful bursts of light. The fun lasted several hours and made me a hero in the neighborhood for a week. That notoriety was important to me because I wasn't well-liked. I was small and weak and didn't play sports very well. You know how cruel kids can be. In Coaltown, if you're not an athlete, you're nothing." Something about Ham told me he was an outsider, too, but I couldn't put my finger on it. I guess that's why I didn't hesitate to run on so.

"Sometimes the hurt can be caused by something pretty subtle. For instance, there was this kid like me in the neighborhood, only even less popular. Once when all the guys ordered Tom Mix decoder rings through the mail, by sending in a top off a Ralston cereal box to the company that sponsored the Tom Mix radio adventure program, every kid on the block got excited when a kid's ring arrived. But nobody got excited when his came." At this point I stopped talking because there seemed to be so much self-pity in it all. We both fell silent for a moment. I don't know what he was thinking, but I was angry with myself for rambling on about my ruptured childhood. But I didn't stop for long.

"My family's very secretive. My parents never tell me what's going on, and I have to figure out everything for myself. It makes me feel lonely and shameful, as if what I think or feel doesn't matter to them. I guess they think they're saving me from worry. They don't seem to realize that not knowing is worse. I get anxious and depressed, which is probably why I bite my fingernails." And I kept it up!

"You know how little kids sometimes act out when they're anxious or unhappy? I turned inward. I shut down. I kept to myself. I spent a lot of time in Grandmom's attic. I dressed up in costumes I found. There was Uncle Fred's World War I uniform, Granddad's old black frock coat, and what I couldn't find I improvised out of leftovers Mom discarded from her sewing. The one thing I couldn't hide from was school. I didn't study, and I was always on the brink of failure. In the early years my teachers pushed me along to the next grade, which made it easy to ignore reality, until I got to high school, and it all caught up with me."

Ham was still lying on his bed, his eyes fixed on the ceiling. I thought he was day dreaming or falling asleep, but he turned to me and said softly, "You really did fail your senior year, didn't you?" It was the first time anyone said it, it didn't make my cheeks burn.

Ham wouldn't talk about himself, which I tried to get him to do, just to get even. Whenever I asked, he gave me short, abrupt answers.

"What's your father do?"

"President of Pridwell Steel."

"Who's the pretty girl in the photo on your desk?

"A girl I was engaged to once. Ah, by the way, Bessie Watty's giving you the eye, Robbatch."

He would change the subject in the middle of a question. He was telling me that June Jamison, who plays Bessie Watty in *The Corn Is Green*, had a crush on me. "Haven't you noticed how she's been hanging around backstage when you're on call?"

This wasn't true, but when I challenged him, he changed the subject again. Once when I was determined not to be put off and returned to the question I'd asked him, he got angry.

"I'm the Grand Inquisitor, not you!" he snapped. He quickly recovered his composure, put his arm around my shoulder and said, "When I finish my book about you, then it'll be your turn to ask, okay?"

Ten

February was a very busy month for me, what with rehearsals in Williamstown and my school work, even though I was taking bonehead subjects that required little attention. The subject that kept me really busy was Theater, which was okay with me; I even did extra work that wasn't assigned, like build a model stage and miniature sets for plays we read.

Miss Marlowe assigned Shakespeare's *Hamlet.* We had to read a few scenes each night and discuss them next day in class. The only Shakespeare I'd read before was *As You Like It,* back in ninth grade. At that time the fancy language really turned me off, but this time I was determined not to let it stand in my way. I found I could understand most of the lines, when I concentrated real hard, and Miss Marlowe translated the hardest parts; I did as well as anyone in the class and better than some. I liked *Hamlet* because I identified with the prince. He had trouble with his mom and step-dad—they murdered his dad! Just the fact Prince Hamlet was young and troubled about his parents, like me, would have been enough to keep me interested. Making it even more interesting was the announcement in school one day that Lawrence Olivier's movie production of *Hamlet* was going to be shown at the Nuluna, and there would be a special matinee, and students would be excused from school to see it.

You know how when you read a play or a story, or hear it on radio, you try to visualize everything in your head, what the characters look like and how they act, and all? Well, this was the first time I saw on the screen something I'd read beforehand. As I watched, I compared it with my ideas. What a revelation that was! Olivier's images were so much better than mine. And he introduced little props, like a little dog he pets gently in one scene when something important is being said. Speeches I'd had trouble understanding were so much clearer when the actors spoke with conviction and used gestures and proper inflection. And there was background music, too, that heightened the drama. I was so impressed I bought the record album of Olivier reading the soliloquies. I've listened to them so many times I know them by heart.

There was one scene in particular in *Hamlet* that really got to me. Hamlet goes to his Mom's bedroom to accuse her of helping his uncle murder his dad. How he knows they did it is because his dad's ghost came back from the dead and told Hamlet. He's horrified that she could kill her own husband, the king, who Hamlet says was so much more of a man than his uncle. And then he accuses her of being tempted by the devil into having sex with her brother-in-law. And then he asks her this question—how can there be shame in a young man's lust when older people who are supposed to be wise and good, but are just as eager and will do anything— even commit murder and have immoral sex?. I'd sure like to know that, too.

After we read and discussed the play, Miss Marlowe had us write an essay about it. I chose to write about the fathers—Hamlet's noble father who was killed, Ophelia's father who was silly and kind of pompous, and step-dad Claudius who conspired in murder. They were contrasting father-figures, and I thought they made an interesting study. Miss Marlowe gave me an A on my essay because she said it showed original thinking, but she questioned the validity of my thesis, which said that maybe Shakespeare had a troubled relationship with his own father, and that's why he portrayed them as he did.

A week or so after *Hamlet,* Miss Marlowe announced one day that a mother of a classmate had reserved a block of tickets to a stage production of *Medea*, starring Judith Anderson, in Pittsburgh. It was a matinee and we'd be excused from school. She told us *Medea* was an ancient Greek tragedy by Euripides, that it was based on a myth about a sorceress who helped Jason get the Golden Fleece, and later when he deserts her, she kills their children to get even. That sounded pretty grim to me, but I wanted to see it. Six of us kids squeezed into this kid's mom's car and made the trip to Pittsburgh.

This play had some pretty strong stuff in it. Medea grabs her breasts and shakes them at the audience—she really did that! And when she talked about killing her kids it was a real eye-opener! The whole play was intense, and I was glad when it ended. Not even the Saturday adventures I saw at the Gable had such strong stuff.

Another new experience I had about this time was seeing a ballet, a movie version of the ballet *The Red Shoes*. It too was offered to students at a matinee. Mostly girls went this time. The only reason I went was to get out of school, but I really did enjoy it. If I'd been made to sit through it, like some of the movies Mom had made me see with her over the years, I'd have been bored out of my skull. The same for Shakespeare and Euripides. It's funny what a new look on life will do. Everything about everything changes when something arouses you from the doldrums. When I told Ham about *Hamlet, Medea,* and *The Red Shoes* he laughed and repeated his disbelief in my "naiveté," as he called it.

When *The Corn Is Green* reached dress rehearsal, I was impressed with how well it all came together: sets, costumes, makeup, lights, and everybody knowing their lines. Some of the adults had been chosen for their roles because they spoke Welsh without an accent. To help us kids, a tutor had been brought in. I have to admit I really struggled with the Welsh, and I kind of drove the tutor crazy, but by opening night I was as ready as I could be.

Even the programs were well done. They'd been printed commercially in color and had photos of the actors who played key roles, along with a list of their credits. There was no photo of me, of course, but under my name it said I was known in Coaltown for my pantomimes, that I read modern poetry, and then these words: "This young man has talent and bears watching." That made me feel pretty good.

Performances were given nightly for two weeks, with matinees on Sundays. On the third night Mom and Dad came to see it. I wasn't sure Dad would show up on time, so I left for the theater in Grandmom's car before he got there. A few minutes before the first curtain I peeked out to see if Mom and Dad were in the seats I'd chosen on the side where I appeared in the first act, my face all black and my clothes dirtied with coal dust.

Right from the first, we all knew it was going to be a good night—the audience laughed at the funny parts and sniffled at the sad ones. Ham had hundreds of lines and appeared in almost every scene. He played his role with great skill and great stage presence, as Miss Marlowe would say. In my second scene I didn't speak. It was a classroom full of young miners of different ages, and me as one of them. Sometimes I pantomimed impudence: I pulled the hair of the girl seated at the desk in front of me, or I tilted my head back, mouth gaping wide, pretending to have fallen asleep. I never played the scene the same way twice. On this night, I picked a fight with the kid who sat at the desk behind me. We wrestled in the aisle, until the teacher came and broke us up. I hadn't told the actor who played the teacher about it beforehand, and I sure heard about it after—I was accused of stealing the scene, which was true, because Mom and Dad were in the audience. Actually, they all liked it and they let me do almost anything, provided I got approval first.

After that performance I took Mom and Dad backstage to meet everybody. Dad made a little speech. Mom coached him. "Ahem, Tucker, I was very impressed. Really, ahem, I think you have talent." And that was all he said. Ham looked my way and winked.

It was late when we got home, and I had to get up early for school, so I said goodnight and went to bed in my roll-away in the dining room. Mom and Dad wanted to talk privately, in the living room, but there was only a wide open arch separating me from them, so Dad left.

When *The Corn Is Green* closed, I was really sad, thinking my work at the Williamstown Playhouse was finished for the year. But when the next production was announced, *The Magnificent Yankee*, and I heard that young men were needed, I auditioned for a part as one of Oliver Wendell Holmes's law clerks, and I was accepted. This time I had a clean face and elegant costumes, including white tie and tails, and lines to speak in English— everybody would recognize me!

In school it was the middle of second semester, and everyone talked about graduation and after. Everyone in Theater class planned to go to college, except me. Ned had applied to Princeton and planned to become a lawyer. Tal, like me, wanted to study acting and had applied to Winchester, a small Presbyterian college close to Coaltown. Its theater program was very small. When I questioned him about this, he said his parents insisted he stay close to home because of his drinking problem. I couldn't understand why a young guy with his brains, popularity, and accomplishments was a boozer.

"Tucker, what are you going to do after graduation?" I was asked repeatedly. Needless to say, I didn't know. I was still stuck in my dumb rut of never thinking ahead. My excuse was, I was too busy getting through the day. It did look like I was going to graduate, and I knew I'd have to decide. I didn't like to bring it up with Mom; she always gave me the old I-told-you-so line. She dropped hints about me going to work in the family business, the Reimer Manufacturing Company. The president was her cousin, and she was sure I'd be given a job, most likely common labor. Dad approved, because after high school he had worked a year in Coaltown Steel beside his dad, the machinist, and earned enough money to pay for his freshman year at Michigan, in Ann Arbor.

I was opposed to this. Failing had already cost me a year. Leaving high school at nineteen, working a year in the factory. What would come after? College? Out of the question! But if I didn't come up with something, for sure I'd be put to work in the factory.

Ever since the big discovery that I was a pretty good actor, I'd secretly considered going to New York or Hollywood and trying to break into the big-time world of the movies, until Ham told me about schools of acting and named some. So one night after a rehearsal of *The Magnificent Yankee*, I talked it over with André.

"There's the American Academy of Dramatic Arts in New York," I said.

"Good enough, but you could choose better. The Neighborhood Playhouse School of the Theater."

I'd read a list of schools in New York, but this was not one of them, and I was skeptical. "Where's that?" I said, scornfully.

"New York." He was a little taken aback by my tone of voice. "Only the most highly recommended are accepted. Fifty in the first year class. The second year class has only twenty-five, because those who make little progress in the first year are eliminated. To apply for admission you must be recommended by someone they respect. I'd be happy to write a letter for you." Still taken aback by my attitude, he said. "Maybe you have a better idea!"

Mom wasn't impressed either. "Such a common name. Sounds like amateur theater to me." She thought about it for a moment and then said, "but if André recommends it, it's worth looking into. There's no harm in sending for details."

Two weeks later a catalog came in the mail. Unlike college catalogs that were thick books, it had only ten thin pages, stapled together under a rather plain cover. It described the program, which included eight hours a day of classes in acting, dance, and speech. Acting was taught by Sanford Meisner, a founding member of the Group Theater. I'd read about him; he was mentioned in my theater class textbook! And the Group theater, too! And then Mom saw who taught modern dance—Martha Graham—the most famous dancer in America! And guess what? At the top of a list of names of graduates who had made it big was none other than—Gregory Peck! That was all Mom needed to give her stamp of approval. Dad, though, had to be sold, and I had doubts about him going for it. An hour-long telephone call between them resulted in his coming for a visit.

"Suppose you're not accepted?" he said.

I knew this would be the sixty-four dollar question. "There are other schools, like the American Academy of Dramatic Arts and the Stella Adler Studio, both in New York."

He thought for a moment and then said, sarcastically, "College should be the subject of this talk, but you know that's not possible." I think he'd always wanted me to go to his alma mater, Michigan. I was sure he'd say something about me going to work in the factory, but he surprised me.

"There's no harm in trying. Write to this school André recommends and ask for an interview the first of next month. I need a reason to visit New York, anyway." It was the first time Mom and Dad made a decision about me that didn't provoke an argument. I filled out and mailed the application that came with the catalog and asked for an interview the first week in April.

I was skeptical about my chances of getting in, but I didn't let it bother me; I had plenty to keep my mind occupied, and I didn't worry about the cost either, or even where I might live in New York. I figured Dad would not have agreed if he didn't have the answers.

Eleven

"Are you sure you have everything, Tucker? You didn't forget your new dress slacks, did you?"

"Everything! Extra socks! Extra shirts! Extra underwear! And I did remember my new pants!" Whenever we traveled anywhere, which wasn't very often, Mom had to make sure I took just about all the clothes I owned.

Dad was waiting in the car, drumming his fingers on the steering wheel. I kissed Mom good-bye, dumped my stuff in the trunk and took my place on the front seat. Mom was not making the trip, which surprised me. I thought she'd want to see the school where I hoped to spend the next two years. She didn't say why.

The first leg of the trip would take us south on nineteen to Pittsburgh, about two hours. From Pittsburgh we would take the turnpike to Harrisburg, about four hours. I always measure distance in time rather than miles. All I ever want to know is how long I'm going to have to sit and be bored.

Pittsburgh was as smoky as ever. Dad had to turn on the headlights, even though the sun was shining. In the distance, along the shores of the Ohio River, I could see thousands of lights winking eerily in the smoke, floating out of the miles and miles of mills and foundries. They had a ghostly kind of beauty, like stars in a dense gray sky. Big sounds filled the air—the roar of blast furnaces, the clank of heavy metal being moved about, steam engines and power equipment. Southeast of Pittsburgh the air cleared and we entered the Laurel Mountains. Looking at a road map, I could see we would continue southeast, tunnel through the Allegheny Mountains, and then the turnpike would swing northeast. We would have to pass through Harrisburg and Allentown on the way to New Jersey. City traffic would slow us, but at least there would be a change of scenery. After that the Lincoln Tunnel and then Manhattan. We had left Grandmom's at seven, so I guessed we'd arrive at seven in the evening.

I settled down for the long ride and made myself comfortable. Twelve hours! New York City and my interview with Sanford Meisner at the Neighborhood Playhouse School of the Theater. I knew this would be a repeat of the trip to Chicago. Dad and me sitting mum and glum the whole way, so I'd brought along a book to read, a collection of plays Grandmom had given me for my birthday. I opened it to *The Skin of Our Teeth* by Thornton Wilder and read.

This was my second trip to New York City by car. The first when I was four, in Granddad's car, with Dad driving and me standing the whole way. We were returning to New York after a visit to Coaltown. Mom still talks about that, how I stood for twelve hours. She thought I didn't want to miss any of the scenery. The truth was, the seat was so crowded with adults I felt smothered when I sat.

It's funny what you remember about a place. Of course, I have no memory of the street in Brooklyn where we lived when I was born, because we moved soon after to Jackson Heights. Mom said once the Brooklyn address was 95th Street in Bay Ridge. It's right where the Lower Bay of the Hudson and East Rivers empty into the Atlantic Ocean. Mom says she used to wheel me along the ocean-side boardwalk in a baby carriage the summer after I was born, but they moved to Jackson Heights. Someday I'll take the subway and go there, just to see what it's like. It's important to me to do that, but I don't know why.

By the way, I almost didn't survive my birth—it was January and the furnace in the hospital broke down, and when I was only a few days old I caught a bad cold and the doctors told Mom I might die, so they had me wet-nursed by a woman who'd had a baby at the same time, and the antibodies in her milk, they say, is what saved me. Often, Mom says throughout my life I've survived more than one scare because God has a purpose for me—I'd sure as hell like to know what it is!

When I think about my life as a little kid age three or four in Jackson Heights, it's all silly little things that I remember, like the little black and white tiles that covered the bathroom floor. Or the iron penny bank that sat on the desk in my bedroom. Or my chenille bedspread covered in sailboats, ropes and anchors. Why do I remember that? Or summer playground program, and we had to take naps on cots in the afternoon. I guess I remember that because I hated the playground—and the feeling I'd been dumped there every day and maybe abandoned.

About supper time we cruised into Manhattan through the Lincoln Tunnel that ran under the Hudson River. I thought of all those tons of water flowing overhead and was glad when the whirr and rumble of the tunnel ended and we emerged into the asphalt and neon of the city streets. I hadn't thought to ask Dad about our hotel. "The Piccadilly on Times Square. Thought you'd like to be in the heart of the theater district," he said, as we swung into Forty-second Street.

"Piccadilly?"

"It's English, a street in London, named for a woman who lived in the Elizabethan Age. She was the best-known maker of piccadills, high lace collars worn by men and women." Dad sometimes surprised me with the trivia he knew, the only kind of stuff he ever passed on.

"Why is a New York hotel named for a London street?"

"I thought you'd ask that. I don't know. There are lots of places in New York with British names. It's snob appeal, I guess."

The Piccadilly was not a fancy hotel, but there was lots of activity in the lobby and our room was clean. "I suppose you'd like to have dinner at Dempsey's." Dad always thought he knew what I wanted without asking, or it was what he wanted to do, but made it seem like it was my idea. Dempsey's was owned by some old heavyweight boxing champion, before my time.

We strolled along Broadway, under thousands of winking, blinking lights racing crazily around the corners of huge marquees and billboards, turning night into endless day. There was one enormous billboard that showed a guy blowing huge cigarette smoke rings—honest-to-god real smoke rings blew out of his wide open mouth every couple of seconds! And the street was so crowded with people hurrying to get somewhere, we nearly got bumped off the curb.

"Where's everybody going?"

"It's curtain time," Dad said.

Every Broadway intersection we crossed had a side street with live shows. Some marquees stood so close to each other they almost touched. There was *South Pacific* with

Mary Martin, *Streetcar Named Desire* with Marlon Brando, *Mister Roberts* with Henry Fonda, *Death of a Salesman* with Lee J. Cobb. All the great shows I'd read about in *Theater Arts.*

Dempsey's was disappointing. The place was crowded, Dempsey himself was nowhere in sight, and his burgers and fries were first round losers.

My appointment with Sanford Meisner was set for ten o'clock in the morning. We had breakfast in the hotel coffee shop. My eggs came with hash browns, which I pushed aside. I don't know how New Yorkers can eat greasy potatoes at breakfast. After, we took the Times Square shuttle train to Lexington Avenue, transferred to an uptown train that took us to Fifty-third Street, and then walked the remaining two blocks, with Dad urging me to remember how we got there, in case this turned into a daily journey for me.

The school stood in a quiet residential neighborhood of five-story town houses, and was itself a town house almost indistinguishable from the others. Its front was painted dull gray, and a modest little sign over the door announced its name under the masks of comedy and tragedy. I was disappointed; I expected something a bit more theatrical. Just inside the front door a receptionist took our names and told us to wait in the lobby. This was a room with black and white tile floor, furniture of steel tubing and black leather, all very sleek and modern. The walls were covered in black and white glossy photos of stage sets and actors in scenes.

"Look here," Dad said, "that's Gregory Peck. He must have been a teenager when this photo was taken." All the photos held familiar faces, though we couldn't put a name to all of them.

Behind us an elevator door slid open and several young, excited bodies emerged, dressed in leotards and ballet shoes. They had towels around their necks and gave off such energy that I thought they must have just come from a dance class. From behind them stepped a man I judged to be about Dad's age, maybe a little younger, and certainly a lot fresher looking. He was tall, had a high forehead, and wore horn rims. "How do you do," he said, "I'm Sanford Meisner." He didn't smile. He spoke very slowly, enunciating each word very carefully, like you might expect of an actor. He wore a very smart summer jacket. Like André, he was elegant and self-assured. I couldn't help notice how different he was from Dad. He studied us very carefully. "Every visitor is attracted to that photo. Peck came to us just after the war. Didn't have a cent to his name. We helped him find a job. Elevator operator at Radio City. He borrowed five dollars from me—and never paid it back."

He led us into the elevator, and from there to his office, a room sparsely furnished that didn't seem to see much activity. "André Swan believes you have talent, Tucker. Why do you want to be an actor?"

"Well, Mr. Meisner, it all started about four months ago, when I did a couple of pantomimes at a New Year's Eve church party. I did Red Skelton and Charlie Chaplin, and everybody said I was terrific. Later, I played Robbart Robbatch in *The Corn Is Green* and a law clerk in *The Magnificent Yankee,* and I did a few one-acts in high school." Until now I had always been proud to speak of my work, but suddenly the insignificance of it all hit me. Oh, my God, I thought, he must think I'm just a small town jerk who's had no real experience and has no sense of where he is at this moment. The reality of it all! This was the *real thing*! This was Gregory Peck's acting teacher I was telling my silly history to!

"How old are you, Tucker?"

"Nineteen. I was sick and they held me back a year." Dad winced.

"You know, don't you, most of our students have had at least two years of college?"

"Yes, but I don't want to go to college. Colleges don't really teach acting, they're academic places. At this school I'd be taught *real* acting by *real* actors. Ever since I got interested, I haven't thought about anything else. Every minute of every day I think about how I'd play certain roles, like Tom Wingfield in *Glass Menagerie*. And I read plays. I've read everything Eugene O'Neill wrote and Arthur Miller and Henrik Ibsen, and now I'm even reading Shakespeare on my own, and—"

"Ahem." Dad stopped me in mid-sentence, and it's a good thing he did, because I'd begun to ramble, being as nervous as I was—burning to make a good impression. And desperate! I was about to tell him I'd prepared an audition for him, the opening scene in *The Glass Menagerie,* when Tom faces the audience and tells them about himself. It's the Depression, they're poor, and like his father, Tom had abandoned his mother and sister, who depended on him for support, because the mother's expectations for him and his sister Laura are unrealistic. He feels he's been driven away, but he feels guilty. In the opening scene, he's come back, he's guilty, he's angry, he's antagonistic. His opening lines are, "Yes, I have tricks in my pocket, I have things up my sleeve, but I'm the opposite of the stage magician—" Tom hurls these words at the audience. I chose this scene because I knew I could use *my* anger and *my* guilt to give the scene the emotion it needed. And I was ready!

"Mr. Amory, may I ask what you do for a living?"

"I sell commercial refrigeration. I own a small franchise in Columbus, Ohio."

"If the theater hadn't beckoned, I'd have gone to work in my father's fur shop," Mr. Meisner said, smiling.

And they went on like this, for about ten minutes, laughing and talking about *themselves*! How could they talk about such dumb stuff at a time like *this*!

"Is Coaltown in Bucks County?"

"On the other side of Pennsylvania, the Ohio side."

"How far is that?"

"About four hundred miles."

"Really! I've done summer work at many theaters around Philadelphia and New Hope, so I think of Pennsylvania as Broadway's back yard. I didn't realize it was so large." Before I could say that I'd prepared an audition, Mr. Meisner got up and ushered us out, saying, "Thank you for coming, Tucker, Mr. Amory. You'll receive a letter from us in a week or so. Have a safe trip home. And say hello to André for me." He spoke without a smile or a hint, and I felt devastated.

On the way back to the hotel, Dad said bluntly, "You're too young, he's not going to accept you."

By the time we got back to the hotel, I was resigned to it. Being here in New York, surrounded by the real theater world, changed everything. I didn't even consider visiting any of the other acting schools. How could a jerk like me make an impression in a big city like this? I'd go back home and spend the rest of my life making furnaces.

I was ready, right then, to go back home, but dad had tickets to *Mr. Roberts*. That night, sitting in the theater, watching Henry Fonda perform with style and grace and conviction, just a few feet away from my seat, brought more discouragement. All the professional actors in this play were so much more talented and poised than the amateurs I worked with. It was *truly* a different world. I could not see myself ever taking part in a Broadway play. Me? Performing in front of a sophisticated New York audience? Who would ever write a review of me? I'd never spoken more than a dozen lines on stage, except for a lead in a silly one-act high school melodrama!

The next day Dad went to see people he did business with. I spent the day walking the streets and riding buses. I window-shopped, sat on a bench in Rockefeller Center, and rode double-deckers up and down Fifth Avenue. That night we saw T.S. Eliot's *The Cocktail Party.* It had a reputation for baffling the audience, and I knew we would not understand it. Some guy dressed in a pin-striped suit sat at a desk and talked across it all night to some dumb lady dressed in silks and furs. Nothing ever happened. Just a lot of sitting and talking. But T. S. Eliot was considered a big-time poet and intellectual, so audiences showed up—just so they could say they saw it.

We drove back home the next day. A week went by, and the letter didn't come. I didn't even bother to look for it in the mail. I knew what it would say.

Twelve

After the disappointing trip to New York, everything else in my life turned sour, too. In school my Sales and Merchandising teacher, Mr. Rockapalumbo, told me I was in danger of failing, I got kicked out of homeroom for mouthing off to the teacher, I had a run-in with Feralman that got me sent up before the school board for expulsion, and at home I discovered Mom had a secret boyfriend!

It had looked like an easy class. What with retail business being in my family, I had signed up for Sales and Merchandising back in September, as I said before. I was kind of interested because of Dad being a salesman and Mom's dad, before he died, an owner of retail stores. In this class we had lots of projects, like collecting labels from canned goods, clipping ads from newspapers, interviewing owners of retail stores, and visiting various businesses. To show what we had learned and to prove we'd made lots of visits, we had to write reports. Well, I have to say, I hadn't done a lot of it. Rehearsals at the Playhouse had taken a lot of my time, and the things I did with Sock and Buskin and Theater class. I had thought I was doing all right, just enough to get by, but Mr. Rockapalumbo said if I didn't get on the ball and make up the back work he was going to fail me.

Then one morning in homeroom I signed out during activity period to go to the boys room. We were only allowed five minutes, but I took ten. When I got back, Gussie let me have it. (Real name Augusta Gibbs, Latin teacher) "There's no earthly reason for taking so long!"

I hadn't done anything wrong. It had just taken me that long to go, and I got angry. "You want to hear all the details?" I said, with more of an edge than I intended.

"Tucker Amory, I'll not tolerate your insolence. Explain the details, if you please, to Mr. Feralman! Go!"

This was my third trip to the assistant principal's office since September. "Well, now, Mr. Amory, what have we here?" he asked in the sarcastic tone he'd taken with me ever since my long absence from English class had caused him embarrassment.

"Ten minutes, that's all, and when I got back she called me for being late, so I asked her if she wanted to hear the details. That's all I said."

"Are you sure this happened this morning; you haven't been hiding somewhere for a month, have you?"

"No, sir, I mean yes, sir." I said, trying not to be angry.

"You were insolent, weren't you?"

Shuffling papers on his desk, pretending to search for something, all the while playing very cool and making it obvious he had me behind the eight ball, he said, "You owe Miss Gibbs an apology, don't you?"

Him sitting there, tilted back in his squeaky swivel chair, hands folded neatly, twiddling his thumbs, all holy and righteous, like he was God or something, brought out the worst in me. "No, I *won't* apologize! I did nothing wrong, and you can't *make* me!"

Leaping to his feet, he roared, "Three days! I want you out of here for three days! And when you come back, you'd better have your parents with you! Collect what you need from your locker and leave, now!"

I stopped at my locker only long enough to get my coat and slam its metal door loud enough to wake the dead, asleep in class.

This time I would have to tell Mom the trouble I was in—and be careful how much I told her, because she still didn't know anything about me getting kicked out of English class and hiding in the library. So I rehearsed my story on the way home: "I didn't do anything wrong, but Gussie threw me out of homeroom and Feralman threw me out of school, so I came straight home."

I drew a deep breath, yanked open the front door and stomped into the living room, ready to tell my story. Two heads popped up from the sofa. Mom was sitting very close to a strange man, and something about it alarmed me. Jumping up, she said, "Tucker, what are doing, coming home so early, in the middle of the morning?" Her voice was very tense, and she stammered a little when she said, "I want you to meet George Roper, a friend of mine."

I shook hands and looked him over. He seemed several years younger than Mom—medium height, medium weight, and completely bald.

"George and I have been friends for many years." Every word she said was supposed to assure me that nothing was going on, but every word said just the opposite. I had met her men friends before. Sometimes some old guy would appear out of nowhere who she'd dated before she married Dad. She'd introduce me, and it would all seem casual and innocent. They would laugh about old times—but this time it was different. "George lives on Case Avenue, with his mother. We often see each other in town, and sometimes we have coffee in Deneen's."

"I'll go now, Sarah, I have an appointment with a client at ten. Pleased to meet you, Tucker, I'm sure we'll meet again," he said, his eyes reaching out to Mom.

I was curious about this guy, but my problem was more urgent. I explained my coming home early. Mom listened, but with her mind still on my stumbling in on Baldy's visit. I gave her my little rehearsed explanation.

But still thinking about Baldy, she said mechanically, "Mr. Feralman wants to see us in three days?"

"Yes, and I think that means Dad, too."

"I'll call him tonight,"

I turned to go, to change out of my school clothes, but she stopped me. "Tucker, before you go, I want to explain about George."

I dropped into the big chair, and she sat on the edge of the sofa across from me, very stiff and upright, with her hands folded tightly in her lap. "George and I met before the war, when you were in grade school. When we lived in Chicago during the war, George was in the South Pacific. We exchanged letters." She took a deep breath and continued, "You know your father and I have had long separations. It's been very lonely. I met George two years into the first separation. You remember, don't you, when your father lost his job in New York and the two of us moved in with Grandmom? It was two years after that."

While she talked, I added up the years. She'd been seeing this George for six years and had corresponded with him for three. That came to nine years, altogether. "Does Dad know about George?" It bothered me only a little that she was seeing someone. Dad was unfaithful, so I could hardly blame her. When we lived in Chicago, Dad's returning home with lipstick on his face, drunk and bragging loudly about the women he'd been with all evening often woke me in the middle of the night.

"Yes, your father knows. About a year ago George brought me home from a dinner date. When we pulled up in front, your father was sitting in his car across the street, waiting. He had come for a visit unexpectedly, and finding only you and Grandmom at home, got suspicious. As soon as he saw us, he left. There was no confrontation. Several months passed. When next we talked, I told him George was just a friend. He didn't believe me.

"Is it just a friendship?"

"George wants me to get a divorce and marry him, but I don't know what to do."

"Does Dad want a divorce?"

"He hasn't said, Tucker. We don't talk about it." What did they talk about? What did they want from each other? What was this crazy marriage all about, anyway? Fighting all the time. Separated four and five years at a time. Neither asking for a divorce. Mom stringing Baldy along for nine years, and Dad with his job-hopping and girl friends. I wanted answers, but I was afraid to ask.

"I must tell you that George has been very generous with you, over the years. Do you remember how badly you wanted a bicycle for Christmas when you were ten? I couldn't afford it, so George bought it for you."

A flood of mixed feelings suddenly welled up in me—anger because I hadn't been told before, gratitude to a stranger who bought me the most important gift I'd been given back then, and guilt because I couldn't be grateful to someone I didn't even want to know. "What else has he done for me that I don't know anything about?"

"A lot of little things he's given you, through me, that I can't remember at the moment."

"And you let him do it! It wasn't me he did it for, it was for *you*!" I shouted. "He doesn't care anything about me! How could he! He doesn't even *know* me!" The words caught in my throat and I started to cry. This, on top of everything else, was too much.

"Oh, Tucker, I've wanted to tell you about George, but you were too young to understand, and then I was afraid."

"Well, I'm not too young now! You never would've told me at all, if I hadn't walked in on you just now!" Mom reached out to me, but I jumped up and ran out of the house. I ran until I was out of breath. Gasping for air, I dropped onto the bench in front of Little Iggy's Café on State Street and struggled to sort out my thoughts about that crummy day. Why does everything have to go wrong all at once?

When I got home, about midnight, Mom and Grandmom were in bed. Mom had left a light on and a note on the table under it. "Your father will be here tomorrow night, Tucker. I phoned Mr. Feralman and made an appointment for the three of us to talk about your suspension."

I spent most of the next day in a corner of the basement I'd fixed up, so I'd have a place of my own in the house. It was furnished with stuff I'd found in the attic: an old rug, a big over-stuffed chair that once stood in the living room of the house where Grandad and Grandmom lived before he died, an old oak table, to hold my phonograph and a stack of old, scratched jazz era seventy-eights. I liked the old hollow sound they produced, and the tinny voices. I had a few books too, and my *Hamlet* records.

Dad came at supper-time. I didn't know what to expect. He'd never had to deal with my problems in school before now. I explained the problem. At first he said very little, and then he seemed impatient.

"You're sure you said nothing more than—'I didn't do anything wrong'?"

"Yeah."

"And he suspended you because you refused to apologize?"

"Yeah."

"Are you sure there isn't something you haven't told us?"

"Nope."

"Then this should be very easy. You'll apologize to Miss Gibbs and Mr. Feralman, and that will be the end of it." He got up from the dinner table and put on his coat. "This is what I had to drive all the way from Columbus for?" He left the house, saying he was going to spend the night at Nanna's and that he'd see us in the morning.

Carrying dirty dishes, I followed Mom into the kitchen, "What's he going to say to Feralman?"

"I'm not sure, Tucker, but you needn't fear that he'll say anything out of place."

In bed that night I lay awake a long time worrying about how all this might affect my chance of graduating—Only juvenile delinquents and half-wits got kicked out of school! And if I didn't graduate would I be given a chance at anything? I probably wouldn't even be given a job at Reimer.

Feralman's secretary announced us. He came out of his office to greet us—all cheery and smiley—a Feralman I didn't know! "How do you do, Mr. and Mrs. Amory, and Tucker, dear boy!" He put his arm around my shoulder and gave me an affectionate tug, "I think we can settle this little problem in no time at all, am I right, Tucker?" Gone was the ever-present frown and deep slouch I'd come to associate with him. Standing tall and erect, arms outstretched like he wanted to embrace Mom and Dad, he ushered us into his inner-sanctum. Seated in his squeaky swivel-chair, grinning from ear to ear, he asked me to repeat the story of my "uncharacteristic behavior," as he called it.

When I finished telling my story, Dad spoke first, "What is Miss Gibbs like, as a teacher?"

Feralman pitched forward and whined, "She's a highly respected teacher, a little old-fashioned, to be sure. She's taught here thirty years, her students love her, and we wish we had more teachers like her." Old Gussie, I said to myself, who brow beats the students she doesn't like. Some students love her because she gives out all the answers before a test, or makes her tests so easy even I could pass them. She will not touch a door handle without first wiping it clean with Kleenex. "Germs," she says, "they are everywhere!"

"Tucker, I want you to apologize to Mr. Feralman," Dad said impatiently, "so you can go back to class."

"You mean, so you can go back to Columbus!" I shouted. And then I did a dumb thing. I didn't even know what I was doing. I leaped across the desk, grabbed Feralman by his lapels, and shook him. "God damn you! I didn't do anything wrong! I was in the boys room only ten minutes, and I'm not going to apologize to you, or Miss Gibbs!" I remember hearing my belt buckle scrape the top of Feralman's desk and my feet leaving the floor as I lunged for him.

"Tucker, for God's sake!" Dad yelled, grabbing me and pulling me away from Feralman. The tightness of his grip on me and my grip on Feralman's lapels turned it all into a three-way wrestling match on top of the desk. Papers, pen holders, and holding trays flew into the air and landed on the floor. It gave me such pleasure to destroy the dead orderliness of the junk he had. Dad finally managed to pull me away from Feralman's lapels, but not before the seams tore open. I collapsed on the floor and burst into tears.

Gasping for breath, Feralman cried out, "Get him out of here! Take him away! Call Mr. Blott! The superintendent will hear about this! You'll pay dearly for this! This is grounds for permanent expulsion!"

Dad pulled me up from the floor, squeezing my arm so hard it hurt, and led me and Mom out of the office. I remember seeing a crowd in the hall, but the only face I could make out was Miss Marlowe's, looking shocked and worried.

When we got to Grandmom's house, Mom and Dad got into a terrific argument about me. "If you were here more often, this sort of thing wouldn't happen! No wonder he's in *trouble* all the time—Every boy needs *a father*! And when are you going to *do something* about the way we live?—The poor boy doesn't even have a room of his own—He sleeps in the dining room, for heaven's sake!"

"I suppose you think I don't know what goes on around here? Does Tucker know about your boyfriend? If he's maladjusted, it's your fault! You're the one who raising him!"

I retreated to my corner in the basement. The fighting went on and on, directly overhead, but I couldn't make out the words. I knew it was over when the front door slammed, telling me that Dad had gone—back to Columbus.

Feralman extended my suspension to ten days. Then there was to be an expulsion hearing, before the superintendent and the school board. I spent most of my time over the ten-day suspension in my corner in the basement, and my evenings at the Williamstown Playhouse. Ham knew something was up, and he prodded me, until I got mad and told him to mind his own business for once. Then I said I was sorry. And then I told him my story.

"Robbatch, if I didn't know you better, I'd say you invented this tale of the prodigal son."

"What do you know, Mr. Perfect? Everybody's fair-haired boy! You have everything—money, brains, great school record, a tight family! And what do you really know about me? Only what I've told you! And for all your pretending, I don't think you really care!"

Ham was not affected by my little tirade. We both fell silent for a moment. Finally he said, calmly and quietly, "It's just that you surprise me, that's all. There's more to you than you give yourself credit for. You have brains, and talent, and there's a future for you, but you need to get away from home, away from the people who make you anxious and depressed. You need to leave your past behind and get on with your life."

"How am I gonna *do* that?" If I'm expelled, there will be no diploma for me. And no future. I'd be lucky to get a job in the family business! And nobody would care!"

Ham didn't seem to have an answer for that, and he wasn't about to let me indulge in self-pity. "We've got a show to do tonight, my friend. The Magnificent Yankee needs his law clerks."

Mom grew very depressed, I could tell, because she had a nervous habit of picking at her blouse when something was bothering her, and now she was doing it constantly. There was something she wanted to tell me, but it took about five days for it come out: "Tucker, I've made an appointment for you with Dr. Herzberg, in Williamstown."

"Who's he?"

Twisting a loose thread on her sleeve, she said, "A psychiatrist."

"Why?"

"What you did to Mr. Feralman shows you're out of control."

"I'll think about it," I said, letting her know I didn't like the idea. But the more I thought about it, the more I came to accept it. I was curious, anyhow. Like in the movies.

Scenes where the shrink tries to dig deep into the sick guy's subconscious—psychopathic killer—amnesiac—rich neurotic housewife being driven insane by a husband who wants her committed, so he can run off with a mistress or take her money. I could see myself playing the scene. Me stretched out on the couch, pouring out my life story, and the shrink seated at my head, where I couldn't see him, with a pad and pencil, taking notes! But then there was the serious side to it—like the time I had to have my tonsils out when I was four because I'd had so many sore throats. Dr. Moses said it was time for surgery. It had to be done.

Dr. Herzberg's reception room was furnished with old stuff Mom called antiques, which wasn't my idea of how it should be furnished. "See that spinning wheel in the window, Tucker. Doesn't it look exactly like the one in Grandmom's attic?"

When I was ushered into the office, I looked around for a couch, but there wasn't one. There was a fancy sofa and a couple of upholstered chairs. The walls were papered in a floral design, and everything about it was bright and cheery, like somebody's living room. I didn't even see a desk anywhere.

I expected him to be old and flabby, a beard and maybe a foreign accent, but this guy was young and trim; he could've been an athlete. He greeted me like I was a guest in his home. "Hello, Tucker, how was your trip?"

"Okay."

"Have a seat. Chair or sofa?"

"Don't you want me to lie down on the sofa?"

"No," he smiled, "that's only in the movies." I sat on the sofa, anyway, and he sat across from me in one of the chairs. "Do you like antiques?" he asked. "The sofa you're sitting on is a Chippendale. I bought it in Boston last year. It came from one of New England's oldest homes."

"Uh, huh," I said. "Grandmom has old stuff in her house. There's a grandfather clock about a hundred years old. I learned to tell time by it."

"How nice for you. That's something to cherish and remember, isn't it? Do you have many happy memories of your childhood?"

"Not many," I said. That's what got him started, and his smile disappeared. He started right in to ask me about school, and family, and friends, and girl friends. He asked repeatedly about girl friends. I had the feeling he was trying to find out if I was queer. He asked about how I got along with Mom and Dad, and when I said I didn't, he really pumped me about that. We talked for about an hour, but he never asked me about tearing into Feralman, which I thought was strange. After all, what was I there for? Then he talked to Mom, privately. After, Mom wrote out a check, handed it to the secretary, and we left the office.

On the way home, we didn't speak for a long time. I fiddled nervously with the lock on the glove compartment, and then finally got up enough courage to ask what Dr. Herzberg had said.

"He wants to see you regularly, for a while. He thinks you need therapy." She paused. "Do you think you need therapy?"

"I don't know. What's therapy?"

"I'm not sure, but I think it has to do with helping you to come to terms with your problems and anxieties by bringing you to understand yourself. You'd meet with him an hour per week. He said it would probably take about six months."

"Six months! There really isn't anything wrong with me. I just got a little out of hand because Feralman hates me."

"*Mr.* Feralman, Tucker, show a little respect. She paused again. "I'm not supposed to tell you this, but Dr. Herzberg thinks it was really your father you assaulted."

"What's that supposed to mean? Dad didn't suspend me from school!"

"He thinks it was rage against your father building up over the years. It was really your father you attacked."

I didn't understand that at all, but I didn't know what to say about it, either, so I dropped it. But I did think about it a lot, during the remaining days of my suspension. I did see Dr. Herzberg, for a while, but not six months. And I eventually found out the reason Mom wasn't supposed to tell me why I assaulted Feralman; in therapy I was supposed to come around to seeing it myself. Dr. Herzberg was angry when he found out Mom had squealed on him.

The expulsion hearing was held at night in the superintendent's office. Everything was the same, like the time I was a witness at Bill Spondike's hearing. Dr. Hammond's desk set in a corner of the long, narrow room that was his office; a conference table running the length of the office, surrounded by about a dozen leather-covered executive chairs for members of the school board, and set against the walls hard chairs for visitors and newspaper reporters. Extra chairs had to be found for all the witnesses. Besides Mom and Dad and Feralman, Blott the principal, Dr. Hammond and the school board, my Theater teacher Miss Marlowe, Miss Gibbs, Miss Witherspoon, Dr. Herzberg, Rev. McNab, and even André Swan, whose appearance really surprised me. It was the first time I'd seen André outside a theater setting, and I thought he looked out of place among all the small town folks—in his tweed suit with handkerchief spilling out of the coat pocket, bright red vest with brass buttons, and elegant British manner. After, when I asked Mom how he knew about the hearing, she said she called up everyone she thought might be willing to say a good word. Everybody was there but Ham, because I didn't think to invite him.

Dr. Hammond nodded to Feralman. He started the meeting. I noticed he was wearing the suit he had worn the day I jumped him, its lapels still torn. "Members of the school board and guests, I asked Dr. Hammond to call this special meeting to discuss expelling a student whose behavior in school has turned violent, so violent that he is a threat to the adults into whose care he is placed during the school day. Before I go into the incident in question, I shall review his school record." My record didn't have much to show, except a few tardies, for which I'd received after-school detention, and my failing grades. Missing from the record was any mention of the weeks I'd hidden in the library during English. "Many students are given detention for minor infractions of rules, but Tucker's failing grades are a major issue. It's not because he lacks intelligence—his psychological profile shows he is very bright. For some reason that only he can explain, he is uncooperative, contemptuous, and rebellious toward his teachers."

While he talked about me, I looked around the room at all the people gathered there to discuss my fate, and wondered why all the bother, why all these people should give up an evening of their time to deal with the likes of me. In a way it added to my sense of shame, and in another way it was kind of flattering. I hated the attention, but I loved it, too.

"This young man assaulted me in my office—with his parents present!" Feralman seemed to want to blame them, too. And then he gave the school board all the details. "You all can see how seriously he assaulted me!" And he pointed to his lapels.

Someone on the school board asked Feralman how he conducted himself during the attack. "I was so shocked; nothing like this had ever happened in my office before. I merely tried to fend him off, and then his father pulled him away. But not before several items on my desk were destroyed in the scuffle, among them some valuable school papers that had to be replaced."

"Did it happen just the way Mr. Feralman described it, Tucker?" This question was asked in a kindly way by the only woman member of the school board.

"Yes, Ma'am, Mr. Feralman didn't lie about anything."

"Is there any reason to believe Mr. Feralman has anything to lie about?"

"No, Ma'am." I don't know why I said *lie*.

Next, the witnesses were called to testify. First, Miss Gibbs, oily and simpering, narrated the event in homeroom, which got me sent to the office, in the first place. "He's really a nice boy at heart," she said, smiling sweetly at Mom and Dad. "I am sure he was not his true self." Why is it that some teachers either turn soft, or turn ever harder when it comes to telling their story to other adults?

Miss Witherspoon was next. She recalled the Armistice Day thing, and how well I "comported" myself. Her southern accent was thicker than ever, extra syllables in every word.

Miss Marlowe told the school board I was the "star among stars" in her Theater class. She is one of the most respected teachers at Cruhl High School, and her endorsement brought smiles from everybody and nods of approval. Feralman squirmed in his seat.

Rev. McNab lauded my attendance at church youth meetings, and praised the job I did with the New Year's Eve entertainment, emphasizing how well I took responsibility. He even said, "Tucker is a fine Christian young man whose faith is strong and true." I almost puked!

The last witness to speak on my behalf was André. He gave the longest and most eloquent testimony. Very poised and self-possessed, he seemed to know how to speak to these people in their own way. There was none of the arrogance and high drama that he displayed at the Playhouse when he spoke to actors. He recalled my first audition, and how he knew right off that I had that unnamable something that grips the attention of an audience. He told them that I never missed a rehearsal, and that during snowy winter days when the roads were slippery I drove to rehearsals that I didn't need to attend, and I did so because I was eager to learn. He talked about how politely and respectfully I worked with adult members of the cast, and that everyone was shocked to hear that I was in trouble. He argued that I should not be judged by my deeds in school alone. "I believe Tucker will bring credit to this school and community some day. If you show compassion and forgiveness now, you will do him and the school a great service to the ideals that you all uphold." When he finished everyone sat quiet for a moment; you could feel what people were thinking; even Feralman, the only one whose thoughts were all negative.

Dr. Hammond broke the spell. "Thank you for your testimony, everyone. Members of the school board, it is now your job to render a decision." He turned to the others. "Ladies and gentleman, you are excused, all except Tucker and his parents, and, of course, Mr. Feralman and Miss Gibbs. Anyone who wishes may wait in the hall, along with the Amorys, while the board votes in private and reaches its decision."

In the hall, Mom, with a handkerchief at her nose and sniffling, pleaded with Feralman. "Isn't there something you could say or do to stop them from expelling Tucker?"

"Hardly!" he said. "If they decide to be lenient, they could put Tucker on probation or name a punishment of their own, or both, but it is highly unlikely."

During the day, the hall outside the superintendent's office in the high school was busy with people coming and going, and now at night a dead and empty place, and the silence was noticeable. No one spoke. I could hear a cleaning woman's tin bucket scrape the floor somewhere far off down the hall and see a blade of light reach out of a classroom door.

Fifteen minutes passed. And then we were called back, sooner than anyone expected. Eagerly, Feralman led the way. Dr. Hammond motioned for us to take a seat near his desk, and then he spoke. "Tucker, you have behaved very badly. Your insolence toward Miss Gibbs is inexcusable, and we must insist that you apologize."

"Yes, sir," I said, "I guess I said the wrong thing." I wasn't all that sorry; I still felt I had been wrongly accused because I really hadn't done anything wrong. But Ham had coached me, telling me that it was foolish of me to put my graduation in jeopardy over such a little matter. Too much was at stake, he said.

"I take it that you are going to apologize," Dr. Hammond said.

"Yes, sir."

Then he turned to the more serious problem. "This terrible incident with Mr. Feralman must also be addressed. With your mother's permission, I spoke with Dr. Herzberg in private. He gave me some insight into your behavior, but we want to hear it from you. Why did you assault Mr. Feralman?"

"I don't know, sir. I lost control of myself. It just happened. I was sorry right after I did it. I wanted to go back and apologize, but I knew no words would get me out of such an awful mess."

"Are you ready now, to apologize to Mr. Feralman?"

"Yes, sir."

"Samuel, Mr. Feralman, are you willing to accept Tucker's apology?"

Confident that I would be expelled, and totally unprepared for this turn of events, Feralman sat stunned for a minute, staring at each board member in turn, and then at Mom and Dad. A few beads of sweat shone on his upper lip. He must have guessed what everyone wanted to hear, and he stammered, "All right, yes, yes, say what you must, Tucker!"

"I am really sorry, Mr. Feralman. I don't know what came over me." Then I remembered what Mom had said—that it was Dad I was assaulting. "I was not really angry with you. It was just that so many things had gone wrong that week, especially outside of school."

"Good! Now that that is settled, the board is willing to reinstate you, Tucker," said Dr. Hammond. "However, probation is in order. Any breach of conduct, no matter how minor, between now and graduation, could result in expulsion without a hearing. Is that clear? Mr. and Mrs. Amory, you know what I am saying?"

And then it was over. The meeting adjourned. Feralman, visibly angry, was the first out the door. Mom started to cry again, and I could see tears in Dad's eyes. But there were no handshakes or words of congratulation. I thanked Miss Marlowe and everyone who spoke up for me, even Old Gussie. Mom hugged me, and clung to me for a moment. And then Dad hugged me, too. It was the first in many years, and as he stepped back he seemed embarrassed. And then a moment out of my childhood suddenly popped into my mind—the last time he had hugged me. It was back in Jackson Heights, when Mom and Dad were happy. I was a little kid and Dad rubbed his scratchy day-old beard against my face in a playful way, and though it stung, I hadn't complained. That was so long ago! And now, standing there in the hall outside the superintendent's office, I began to cry, too. I cried all the way home—all the sorrow and anguish of ten long days poured out of me.

It was almost midnight when Dad said goodnight, patted me on the back, and went to Nanna's to spend the night.

Mom, standing in front of the long mirror on the back of the closet door and checking the look of the dress she'd made to wear on Easter Sunday, but wore to the hearing, said, "Tucker, don't lock the front door just yet, I forgot the mail." She stepped onto the front porch, and when she returned held an envelope in her outstretched hand. By the way she looked at me, I knew what it was. Taking a deep breath, she said, "It's come, Tucker, your letter from New York."

I was almost afraid to take it from her. Printed in the upper left corner, in neat black letters, the familiar name and address of the school. In the middle my name and address, neatly typed. With Mom's letter opener, which I had never used, I slowly cut open the flap. The letter was written on stiff, heavy business paper, the expensive kind that's watermarked. The names of the school's sponsors tumbled ladder-like down the left margin: Gregory Peck, John Gielgud, Edmund O'Brien, Helen Hayes, Lawrence Olivier, Elia Kazan, Clifford Odets, and more.

Dear Tucker,

We are pleased to inform you that you have been accepted as a student in the new class, beginning September 24. In a few weeks, you will receive from us a list of things you will need for dance classes. As you know, room and board are your responsibility, but we can advise you in this. If you have any questions before you hear from us again, please call or write.

The letter was signed by the school's director, Mrs. Rita Morgenthau, a name I didn't recognize. But Mom did. "The Morgenthau's are very wealthy. A member of that family is Secretary of the Treasury, in Washington."

When Mom said that, I remembered seeing the signature on dollar bills.

Among my clothes in the bottom drawer of my chest, I had tossed the school's catalog. I crawled into my roll-away and read again what it said about five hundred applicants being interviewed for admission and only fifty being accepted. I wondered what was so special about me. What could André have said in his letter that won my acceptance? What could Sanford Meisner have seen in me, in just a short interview? What did Ham see in me? What did everybody but me see in me? Staring at the ceiling, I puzzled over these questions. Finally, I fell into a deep sleep. When I awoke the next morning, I was startled to find myself looking through a tent-shaped tunnel, and thought I was dreaming. It was the catalog, folded like a tent, standing upright on my chest in front of my eyes.

Thirteen

"Mrs. Morgenthau said she'd advise us about living arrangements. Does he know that?"

"Yes," Mom said, stitching a hem in a skirt.

"So what's he waiting for, anyway?" I paced the floor in front of her sewing table, cursing Dad for keeping me in the dark. "Probably rent a room in a boarding house, at first."

"I suppose so."

"When is he going to let us know? School starts a month from today!"

"Ouch! I don't know, Tucker. Darn, I pricked my finger. Will you please stop pacing, you're making me nervous!"

"I knew this would happen. Left hanging again! Not knowing what he's thinking, until the last minute! And maybe not come through at all. A month from now I'll still be sitting here in Coaltown, and they'll wonder what happened to me!"

"Don't be sarcastic. I'm sure your father knows what he's doing. It's just that he doesn't always tell us," she said, sucking her wounded finger.

"Famous last words! He'd better not leave me dangling again, and then show up at the last minute!" It happened often. There was the time he was going to take me to the rodeo at Madison Square Garden, when I was about five. He didn't come home the night before. He finally showed up in the middle of the day, an hour before the rodeo, and Mom gave him hell as he cleaned himself up, and we just barely made it in time.

She pretended not to be, but Mom was anxious, too. There were late night long distance phone calls, some that lasted past midnight and turned into shouting matches and slamming down of the receiver.

Another two weeks passed. I still didn't know what was up, or even know for sure that he would be taking me to acting school in New York. And then he finally came! No phone call beforehand—he just suddenly appeared!. I was sitting on the front porch reading Eugene O'Neill's *Strange Interlude*, for the second time. I heard a car pull up and turned around—the pink Kaiser—so I knew it was Dad.

"How are you?"

"Fine," was all I said. There was still a coldness between us, and talk didn't come easy.

"Ready for New York?" He said this, as if I was supposed to know what was in his mind.

"Yeah, but—" Before I could finish what I had to say, Mom popped the screen door and interrupted. She suspected I was about to say something stupid, which was probably true. We sat on the wicker porch chairs, and Dad finally told us what we were waiting to hear.

"I've reserved a room for you at the Pickwick Arms on Fifty-third Street, two blocks from the school. That'll do, until you make other arrangements. Ask around. See if classmates are willing to share an apartment, the sooner the better, the hotel costs fifty a week."

"Can you afford that, Roger?" There will be other expenses, too, while he's living in a hotel."

"I've deposited five hundred in a bank near the school. That will cover meals and out of pocket expenses. How long it lasts is up to you, and how soon you find roommates. And maybe a part time job."

"Suppose his classmates have already settled into living arrangements. It's very late to be considering it!"

"We'll face that problem when we come to it!"

I felt a little less anxious, now that things were settled, but I was still pretty upset. I called Ham and told him the good news. I hadn't seen him since the closing of *The Magnificent Yankee.*

"Wonderful," he said. I told you it would all work out. Patience, Robbatch. Your father can be exasperating, but has he ever really not come through?"

I could have said yes to that, but we had other things to talk about. "I've got news, too," he said. "I've been to New York since I saw you last, and I've decided to settle there for a while. You're welcome to move in with me. Share my apartment. How about it?"

"You never told me you had plans."

"Months ago. But I can't talk about it now. What are you doing tonight? I'll drive over to Coaltown. I've not been there before, have I? I'd like to see if all you've told me is really true."

I didn't tell Mom about Ham's offer. I figured he'd have a ritzy place in some expensive neighborhood, and I'd never be able to afford half."

"It's two rooms and a bath in Greenwich Village," Ham said. We were seated in the living room, Ham's eyes giving everything the once-over. He'd never set foot inside a small house in a working class neighborhood before.

I didn't like the look on Mom's face. "Tucker's father won't approve. It's nothing against you, Hamilton—It's the location."

"Why?" dumb me asked.

"I know what you're thinking, Mrs. Amory, but I can assure you it'll be all right. The apartment has been in the Williamstown Playhouse family for years. What I mean is, whenever someone from the Playhouse chooses to live in New York, there is always a place there for him or her to settle into, provided it is available. Well, it became available again, and I've taken it. The rent is only sixty-five a month, including utilities, which Tucker and I would split between us."

"That certainly is reasonable. But money's not the issue—It's that part of the city! I don't think it's healthy."

"What's wrong with it? It sounds like a nice place to me," I said, as if I knew.

"It's not what you think it is, Tucker. It's an old and ugly part of downtown. Some of the buildings don't even have central heat or modern plumbing, and it borders on the Lower East Side. And the people are, well—different."

"What's that supposed to mean?"

"Your mother is saying that residents live a style of life you're not accustomed to."

"Free thinking and free living!" Mom exclaimed. She didn't explain, and Ham didn't seem to want to explain in her presence.

"We'll talk it over with your father. He'll like the low cost."

Ham was still eyeing the room, looking for signs of the way we lived. "That's where you sleep?" He saw my roll-away, where it stood folded against the wall in the dining room. "Hm," was all he said about that.

"I like your grandmother's house. It's simple and honest—no pretensions. He went to the front door and looked out. "Neat and clean neighborhood, and I bet all the neighbors are close. Comfortable little bungalows and white frame houses with front porches. I like that. In my neighborhood, the houses are bigger than anything any family needs. They're spread far apart and neighbors don't speak. Next door complained to the city council once because we had crabgrass, and because I often leave one of our garage doors standing open—unsightly, they said. And believe it or not, there is an unspoken agreement that says one does not hang one's laundry outside in the yard to dry in the sun—it's considered uncouth! Every property is surrounded by a tall fence. Have you ever noticed the wall surrounding the Dewitt estate? It's topped with standing shards of glass embedded in cement!"

I knew everyone who lived in these houses, some who were as Ham said, but also some who did not fit his stereotype. Old Mr. Peters across the street swore at kids, and when the middle-age widow who lived a few doors down asked teenage boys in the neighborhood to do chores for her inside, she stood around and let her housecoat fall open.

"You haven't told me about New York?"

"Think, Tucker. What did I tell you? I want to write, so I've enrolled in a playwriting class at the New School. It's just a block from the flat."

Dad was all for it! Instead of paying fifty a week to a hotel, he'd only have to pay my half—thirty-seven fifty per month. And he didn't object to Greenwich Village. "He's got to grow up sometime, Sarah." So that put to rest my worries of the moment.

In school I made up the work I owed Mr. Rockapalumbo, though it took a lot of help from Ham to pull it off. "I'm appalled at the kind of subjects you're taking! Here we are, cutting out ads from magazines, like girls playing with paper dolls; we should be conjugating Latin verbs or studying photos of Greek temples. No chemistry? No physics? Don't they offer anything of substance at Cruhl High?"

I ignored the questions.

When time came for graduation, I didn't look forward to the ceremonies—They conjured up images of my old classmates graduating without me, and the shame I had felt. Mom wanted me to pose, in my cap and gown, for a photo in Mr. Peters' flower garden, but I refused. I didn't want anyone in the neighborhood to see me. Dad didn't attend baccalaureate, but he did show up for commencement, without telling us he was coming. After, he took us to Sotus's for dinner, Coaltown's fanciest restaurant. I ordered my favorite: roast leg of lamb with mint sauce and mashed potatoes.

After dinner there were presents waiting for me at Grandmom's house: a tartan sport coat from Grandmom, new luggage from Mom, and a very heavy package from Dad that I was told not to open till last, so I knew it had to be something special.

"Not yet," Dad said. He reached out and touched something. There was a faint hum of a motor starting, and then a voice: "Tucker, I know I have not been a very good father. I regret very much that we have not been close. My only excuse is that circumstances have not always been in our favor. I hope that I will be a better father to you in the future. I want to start by seeing to it that you get the kind of schooling you need, to reach the goals you have set for yourself." He paused. "I hope it is not too late to repair the damage that's been done to our relationship—" There was another pause, and a humming that continued for a few seconds. I had a feeling Dad wanted to say more, like he got a little choked up, but then there was a click and the humming stopped. I removed the wrapping from the box, and found to my great delight a tape recorder.

"To help you train your voice," Mom said.

Another day-long, boring trip in the car! But I vowed it would be different this time—no more hours of dead silence between me and Dad. I was determined to talk with him about the crazy life we led. The therapy sessions I'd had with Dr. Herzberg had given me some insight, and I wanted to talk.

You know how when you go to a doctor he diagnoses your sickness and sends you away with a prescription? It's different when you go to a psychiatrist; he doesn't tell you what sickness you have; you do all the talking and discover for yourself what your sickness is, if any. Of course he helps, by asking questions that make you open up about the important things in your life—things you wouldn't talk about with anyone else, not even your parents—especially not with your parents. In therapy, sometimes you find yourself trapped in a corner of your deepest troubles, and the only way you can escape is to face up to them. That happened to me pretty often during my sessions, and I began to see myself a lot clearer. I learned that my absentee father and my weak mother had a lot to do with my personal problems, but I also learned that I had to take responsibility for myself, and that I shouldn't just blame my parents for everything.

There was a lot Dr. Herzberg had wanted to know about Mom and Dad that I couldn't tell him at the time, so I set out to find out, and the trip to New York seemed like the perfect time.

"What was it like for you when you were a boy growing up with Nanna and Granddad? What was it like to have brothers?" I waited till we were past Pittsburgh and cruising on the turnpike to ask these questions. He was kind of caught by surprise. He kept his eyes on the road, and it took him a few minutes to gather his thoughts.

"I was the oldest. Your uncles Frank and Lester and I were two years apart. We were close enough in age to be friends." He paused. "But we were not close. They were very jealous because, as the oldest, I got the best of everything."

"I wonder why I always thought Uncle Frank was the oldest?"

"Probably because he died young, and you never knew him."

"Like with Grandad. I have only vague memories of him."

"You were only five when your grandfather died. Did you know he was born in England? His family followed the old English practice of handing down everything of importance to the oldest son; it's called primogeniture. For instance, at the dinner table. Everything he had to say to his sons was directed only at me, sitting on his right, and Frank and Lester listened in, to whatever they wanted to know. And whenever there was an occasion to give a gift the best was always given to me. My birthday present at thirteen was my grandfather's monogrammed gold pocket watch. It would have been unthinkable to give it to Frank or Lester. And the same was true of any family heirloom."

Dad stopped talking. I could see I'd have to ask everything I wanted to know. But I waited a few minutes before going on. "How come Uncle Lester and Uncle Frank didn't go to college?"

"There was not enough money. They went to work in the steel mill, where your grandfather worked till he retired, and where your Uncle Lester still works to this day."

"How did they feel about that?" Dad didn't answer this question, and I didn't go after it because he was getting very tense. But then he surprised me with what he said next.

"I was spoiled, and I feel very guilty." Dad let out a sigh, and the tension seemed to go out of him. "Everything came easy. I took it all for granted, and, Tucker, I think you are old enough to hear me say this—I sometimes think it accounts for all my weaknesses."

We had just left the turnpike and were entering Harrisburg. He didn't say anything more at this point, and I didn't want to bother him, driving through city traffic. So neither of us spoke for a while. When we reached the outskirts, he surprised me again, picking up where he'd left off.

"Growing up, everything came easy. I didn't study in school or college because I learned very early I didn't have to. In college I made friends with others like me—young men who were fast and arrogant, but some, unlike me, who came from wealthy families. Today, people call it the Roaring Twenties, the age of the flapper and the profligate. Everybody was out to have a good time." He turned, and looking at me for the first time since we started talkng, said, "I'm telling you all this, Tucker, because I want to warn you against making the kind of mistakes I made. You're on your own now. You'll be making new friends. In the theater world, there are all kinds of temptations."

"Yeah, I know. Ham has already told me what to expect in a big city like New York."

"After college I took an executive job in New York, because I wanted to get rich, like everyone in that crazy decade, and fill my life with excitement. And when the Depression struck, like so many people, I wasn't prepared for it. The good times ended. I lost my job with Brasco Glass & Aluminum because I was too proud to take a cut in pay. Why should I? After all, I was the one who won the contract for all the glass and aluminum fascia that covers the outside of the Empire State Building—a multi-million dollar deal! After that nothing was ever right again—because I didn't have the strength, the discipline, or the wisdom to face anything straight on. I haven't held any job for more than three years. I've been unfaithful to your mother, sometimes a drunk, and a spendthrift, all my life."

That was hitting pretty hard. I didn't know what to say, so I changed the subject—I asked about him and Mom.

"I'll be candid with you, Tucker, though you may not like what I have to say. Her growing up wasn't much different from mine. She too was spoiled by her parents, but in a different kind of family. The Reimers were wealthy. Besides the factory there were the retail stores your Grandfather Reimer owned, five altogether, until they were wiped out by spring floods or bankruptcy. Her family had money one year and none the next. He, your grandfather, would have died in bankruptcy, if the factory hadn't taken him back."

"What do you mean, Mom was spoiled?"

"No one ever said no to your mother. Because the family was prominent in Coaltown and she was pretty, she was everybody's darling. Like all of the Reimers, she had talent and often performed in amateur theatricals—she danced and sang and nearly always won the leading role. Everyone told her how special she was, and she came to believe it herself. Then her father died, the big house on Main Street was sold to pay debts, she took a job as retail clerk, the Depression hit. Emotionally, she was unprepared for it all." He paused. "Tucker, I don't want to denigrate your mother, but she too is weak and selfish. Just as I have not been a good father, she has not been a very good mother. That may be hard for you to see. After all, she has always loved you and stood up for you in a crisis. But she hasn't paid attention, day by day. When you were doing poorly in school, where was she? Throughout grade school would you have continually received only barely passing grades, if she had been alert and met with your teachers and insisted you do your homework? Would you have failed senior year, if she had had the foresight to see it? Instead, she buried her head in the sand or escaped into her little dream world filled with fancy clothes."

I wanted to say, where were you when I was growing up? But I didn't want to antagonize him, and, besides, it all seemed to fit with all that Dr. Herzberg's probing into my family's past had dragged out of me. Mom had failed to confront my problems because she was preoccupied with her own troubles, or because she lacked the strength. I hope this doesn't sound like I'm blaming everything on Mom and Dad. As I said before, I take responsibility for my mistakes. But mistakes have to be seen in the context in which they were made, as Dr. Herzberg said.

Some revelations I'd had during the time I was seeing Dr. Herzberg were too sensitive to discuss with Dad. I couldn't tell him, for instance, how much I needed a strong father, and that André Swan had become my surrogate father, during rehearsals when he put his arm around my shoulder sometimes and gave advice or told me I was doing well. Of course, I never told André what all he meant to me—I never felt open enough to make such a confession. But in all he said and did for me, that's what he was, a father. And now it's going to be Sanford Meisner, I hope. He's strong and exacting and trustworthy, like André.

I suppose in a way, I have a brother now, too. Ham watches over me and says he's going to educate me in all the important things: music, art, literature, and stuff.

On the subject of my sessions with Dr. Herzberg, there's something more I have to say.

One day he asked me, "Tucker, has your interest in acting and the time you spend with it changed you in any way?"

"Yeah, I suppose so," I said. "I hang out with the leaders in school, and I'm taking a class that only the brightest get into."

"How do you get on with the teacher?"

"Okay. Miss Marlowe is very good to me."

"And you to her?"

"Sure. I wouldn't think of disappointing her."

"Why?"

"I don't want her opinion of me to change."

"Because you have a better opinion of yourself, and you don't want to lose it?"

I had to think about that, for a moment. "Yeah, I guess you could say that."

"Would you agree that your behavior has changed somewhat because you have a new opinion of yourself? You've discovered a talent, and through it you have gained self-respect. We behave according to the opinion we have of ourselves. If we have no self-respect, our behavior is often negative, for we must do things that confirm our self-hatred. If we have confidence in ourselves, and self-respect, we behave in a positive manner, for that too we must confirm." That gave me lots to think about.

The great thing about my sessions with Dr. Herzberg was that he didn't preach. He asked a lot of questions, and then he led me to logical conclusions from the answers I gave. And when I couldn't find the right words, he said what I couldn't say. After some of those sessions, I began to reflect a lot on my past, and I could see that I did a lot of dumb things, and failed to do smart things, because I hated myself, and though I couldn't see it at the time, the favor I did for Miss Witherspoon, the Armistice Day thing, was the beginning of the new me. And even the work I did in the library for Miss Toomey. Though it's true I wasn't honest with her, I did everything she asked and never mouthed-off, and I felt good about it. I even went back to the library just before graduation, (Miss Toomey finally did let me back in) because I wanted to read again the book the philosopher William James wrote, *The Will To Believe,* where he said that faith makes good things happen. He used an example of a man who climbed a mountain and worked himself into a position from which the only escape was a terrible leap over an abyss. He said that if you have faith that you can possibly make it, and your feet are strengthened by confidence, you *will* make it. And then he said, "But mistrust yourself, and think of all the things you have heard about failure, you will hesitate so long that when you finally launch yourself in a moment of despair, you roll in the abyss." Man, oh man, there were many times I "rolled in the abyss."

Another person I felt pretty grateful to was Miss Marlowe. I suppose I could say she became my surrogate mother for a while. She was kindly, even affectionate sometimes, along with being demanding, insisting I do my best in her class. She not only made me do my Theater homework on time, she kept her eye on me when I left school for home every day and asked what books I was taking with me. (If I turned up empty-handed Mom never said a word.)

But I have to say that I still had trouble understanding how my failing in school was linked to my life at home. Dr. Herzberg told me that I failed senior year because I was trying to draw attention to my needs. But the way I saw it, I was just flat-out bored, and that's why I flunked!

Fourteen

In September Ham and I settled into our flat in Greenwich Village. I was pretty naive in thinking our neighborhood was actually a village. It's a part of the city, pretty much like any other old residential area. We were on the corner of Sixth Avenue and Twelfth Street, one floor up. The ground floor was all Sixth Avenue shops: deli, shoe repair, groceries, and so on. The whole second floor was a huge loft. The landlord, an artist and antique dealer, stored his stuff and did his art work in it. There were sofas, chairs, tables, statues, paintings, stacked all around, and some of it was very strange-looking. Ham knew all about it, and identified periods and styles, like Chippendale, Sheraton and Louis XV. The biggest and fanciest stuff was called Baroque. Rows and rows of it twisted and turned mazelike through the dark. Small stuff, like kitchen chairs, picture frames, and candle stands hung from the ceiling. I mean this loft looked like something you'd see in a horror film, with the dust and cobwebs, and all!

One corner, our apartment, was partitioned off. Ham called it a cold water flat, though it did have hot and cold running water. What it didn't have was central heat. Heat came from a coal- burning fireplace in the combination living-bedroom. We also had a kitchen and a bath. For furniture, the landlord gave us our pick of stuff in the loft. We had twin beds, each set in alcoves in adjacent walls, which during the day served as sofas, with huge pillow backs; a genuine oriental rug, two heavily upholstered Art Deco chairs, drawn up in front of the fireplace, two Edwardian dressers, a spinet desk, and a coffee table made of wooden planks held up by cement blocks—and in the center of it a Russian samovar made of polished brass. The coal-burning fireplace was faced in fancy white marble. On cold nights a good fire burned eight hours without needing attention and kept us warm. It also served for cooking meals, which we ate sitting on pillows, at the coffee table, in front of the fire. On cold nights, we sat in front of the fire, in the big chairs and talked, read, or listened to Ham's records—he taught me all about classical music. His favorite composers were Bach and Mozart, but I prefered Beethoven. We mostly sat in the dark when we weren't reading, because the fire gave off a warm glow, and there was a stained-glass panel in the entrance door that cast another kind of warm glow over the flat.

Our neighbors were mostly artists, musicians, writers, college professors, and people Ham said were *Bohemian*, which meant they had artistic or nonconformist tastes. Most were either very rich or very poor. The rich dressed European, the poor old and shabby—but Ham said that some of the richest look the poorest, and vice versa. They all lived in discrete little flats, tucked away in alleys or muses, and some had lovely little hidden back gardens.

On weekends we went for long walks, and Ham lectured me on the history of Greenwich Village. He said that within a few blocks of our flat lived at one time Thomas Paine, Herman Melville, James Fenimore Cooper, Edgar Allan Poe, Henry James, Mark Twain, and Eugene O'Neill, just to name a few! And many of the oldest houses, dating back to the colonies, were still standing and had been faithfully preserved, or restored to their original glory. Ham showed me a passage in Thomas Wolfe's novel *You Can't Go Home Again* that described Wolfe's Village apartment, located in a building on our street: "He loved this house on Twelfth Street, its red brick walls, its rooms of noble height and spaciousness, its old dark woods and floor that creaked; and in the magic of the moment it seemed enriched and given a profound and lonely dignity." Reading that passage gave me goose bumps, so close was that building to us! It made me want to read the whole novel.

Sometimes at night or on weekends we hung out in one or two of the neighborhood bars; there was the San Remo in McDougal Alley and The White Horse Tavern in the West Village. In both I met a lot of Ham's intellectual friends and writers—at the San Remo an old poet named Maxwell Bodenheim, who in the Twenties was a friend of Fitzgerald and Hemingway. He was a drunk, and would write anyone an original poem who would buy him a shot of whisky. There was a young poet from Swansea, Wales, whose booming voice and habit of pinching girls' bottoms attracted a lot of attention at The White Horse Tavern. And there was a young guy who had written a novel about his experiences in the army during the war in the Pacific. Ham said he was famous already. I mostly just sat and listened to the talk, because they were all so smart and well-educated.

By the way, there's something I have to tell you about Ham. It really doesn't matter, but I'll say it anyway. Shortly after we moved into our flat, he told me he was a queer. At first I was angry, and I told him so. If he'd told me earlier, I wouldn't have moved in. We talked it out and came to an agreement—he could have his boyfriends come to the flat and I'd have my girl friends, and we'd respect each other's privacy. We settled on this because our friendship was bigger than all that, and besides he'd never tried anything funny with me. After he confided in me, I thought about it a lot, and found there were signs all along I should have seen, like the authors he read—so many of them were queers. Anyway, all that too is in the past.

One day, while looking through one of Ham's books, I found a poem that was written by a young Harvard guy named John Reed. In the year 1911 he made his home in the Village and wrote a poem about how he felt about it. I typed a copy and hung it on the mirror over my dresser, because it said how I felt about my new life, among all the Bohemians with whom I felt at home. It went like this:

But nobody questions your morals,
And nobody asks for the rent—
There's no one to pry if we're tight, you and I,
Or demand how our evenings are spent.
The furniture's ancient but plenty,
The linen is spotless and fair,
O life is a joy to a broth of a boy
At Forty-two Washington Square!

It was an old-fashioned poem, for readers of modern poetry like me, in the year 1950—but I liked what it said about being free, even though you're poor, because you have youth and energy and faith in yourself.

For two years I took classes at the Neighborhood Playhouse School of the Theater. On the very first day of the first year, I made a big impression. Mr. Meisner, Sandy, we called him, taught our first acting class. He handed out scripts and had several of us read aloud. But he didn't like anyone's reading. "Relax! You're trying too hard!" he said, and then he'd lean back and take a long drag on his Pall Mall, a pregnant pause, as they say. But everyone looked confused and continued to turn it on. When my turn came, I read the scene easy and conversational, as if I were talking about the weather.

"That's better," he said. "Everyone but Tucker assumed I wanted a performance, which is precisely what I didn't want." He took another long drag, and another pregnant pause. "The first thing you must learn here is how *not* to act." Heads turned, not believing what they had heard. "We start with a clean slate. You must abandon bad habits, and everything you think you learned about acting in college." Was I glad to hear that! I'd worried about my immaturity, my lack of education, and my lack of experience, compared to them, and here he was telling all these smart people that it didn't count for anything. "Tucker is the least experienced and the least trained among you, and that, class, is an asset here."

Speaking of classmates, I met a lot of interesting young people. Some had famous names. Brooks Clift was there, brother of Montgomery Clift; and Anne Pearson, niece of radio commentator Drew Pearson. There was Suzy Sulzberger, daughter of the publisher of *The New York Times*; and Conrad Bromberg, son of movie actor J. Edward Bromberg. Everyone was very sophisticated. In the student lounge, the talk was about politics, art, poetry, and events reported in the daily paper. Some had studied abroad and sat off in a corner by themselves and conversed in French. Many wore black arm bands to school, to show their support for the Rosenberg couple who had been accused of selling A-bomb secrets to Russia. When I got back to the flat at night, I drove Ham crazy, getting me caught up intellectually with everyone. One night, Ham asked me what I knew about the stuff that was happening in Washington, D.C., in hearings of the Un-American Activities Committee, in Congress. Eight Hollywood producers, directors, and writers had been called to testify about their politics. They refused to say whether they'd ever been communists, so they were convicted of contempt. Six were sent to jail. Ham said it was a witch hunt, to gain political advantage for Senator Joseph McCarthy, a Republican from Wisconsin. Ham said the accused had been robbed of their civil rights guaranteed by the Bill of Rights, and that such action threatened freedom of speech guaranteed to all Americans. My classmates at acting school talked about that, too, and had some pretty strong opinions, like Ham, which left me confused, because all the stories in *The Coaltown Times* back home favored exposing communists, wherever they turned up. It puzzled me that smart people, like writers and actors and intellectuals, would be communists. It all came about during the Depression, when many intellectuals had lost their faith in Capitalism and free enterprise, and looked for a different ideology, Ham said. But many of them later came to see the truth about communism, that it was really a form of tyranny, as it was practiced in Russia, and preached a kind of economy that destroyed personal initiative, and so forth. But for a while, I didn't know what to think. Then one day I heard that the father of my classmate Conrad Bromberg had been called to testify because he was suspected of having once associated with communists, and that's when I really got involved in the issue—The more I learned the more I was caught up in it all, and then I too saw them as a witch hunt!

I hadn't known I would learn more than just acting at this school.

Another thing I hadn't anticipated was the way we did acting classes. I'd thought they'd consist of doing scenes from plays. But it wasn't like that, at all. We improvised everything, which means we placed ourselves in an imaginary conflict, or some kind of tension, and then acted it out with a classmate. We spoke our own thoughts, the words arising from the conflict we invented or from the tension we felt—imaginatively. It sounds almost like real life, but it's not. It's kind of complicated, and I don't know any other way to explain it, other than to say it required tremendous concentration. It's called the Stanislavsky Method. For instance, one day I improvised a scene I borrowed from *The Glass Menagerie*. It's the one where Tom loses his temper with his mom. It starts off with her accusing him of being selfish, but the opposite is true: he sacrificed his personal ambition to stay home and care for his crippled sister and mother, who's an abandoned wife, because it's the Depression and they have no means of support, and to help them he's taken a menial job in a warehouse. Tom is so angry in the scene he screams at her, calling her an ugly, babbling old witch. I chose this scene because it awoke strong personal feelings in me. When I got through screaming at the girl who played my mother, I was hot and sweaty and out of breath. Sandy found lots of good things to say about my improvisation, and then the class ended. After the room emptied, I stayed behind to pull myself together. I was alone, the room was very quiet, and I was sitting on my chair with my shoulders leaning forward and my head down, when suddenly this strange thing happened—My life passed before my eyes! Just like the stories you hear about people who find themselves near death! I had flashbacks, images of Mom—all the mean things I'd said or done over the years, in my anxiety and frustration—and a million regrets! And then, just as suddenly as it started, it stopped. It couldn't have lasted more than a few seconds, but it left me shaken and exhausted. I told Sandy about this later in the day. He was alarmed, and told me I was lucky I didn't have a nervous breakdown. After that day, I avoided improvisations that came too close to my own true experiences. I mention all this here so you'll know how intense real acting can be and the concentration it requires.

We also had classes in speech; and we had dance. There was choreography, taught by Nina Fonaroff, a former dancer with the Bolshoi. In this class, we made up dances and then performed for her, while Louis Horst, Martha Graham's music composer, accompanied us on piano. That was a pretty interesting class. But the most exciting class was modern dance, with Martha Graham. I was surprised at what a tiny person she was—only four feet eleven and about ninety-five pounds! But when she talked—and when she glided across the floor in her swirling black silk gown, to illustrate a movement, the room crackled with energy, and she became a giant!

At the end of the second year, we did a family drama called *Call It a Day*. It was about a suburban middle class family. The leading roles, father and mother, were played by Sandy's assistant acting teacher, Jimmy Doolin, and Emily McLaughlin, the oldest girl classmate. My role was teenage son. My best scene was a flirtation in the third act, with the teenage girl who lives next door. She was played by a classmate, a cute blonde with a southern accent named Joanne Woodward. Sandy told her right off she'd have to lose the accent, or she'd be forever type-cast. She dropped it immediately.

Because it was one of our graduation pieces, a special audience was invited—agents, producers, writers, and directors. Clifford Odets, Harold Clurman, Howard DaSilva and J. Edward Bromberg were in the audience one night. The morning after opening night, Joanne Woodward and I received calls from Maynard Morris, actor's agent; he wanted to meet with us real soon. We had interviews and we were supposed to sign five year contracts. I don't know what she agreed to in her interview, but I signed with him.

So, everything would have been great, if there hadn't been something new to worry about! Right after high school graduation in June a war had started—North Korea attacked South Korea. At first, I didn't pay much attention to the stories about it in *The Coaltown Times*, because I didn't think it would affect me. Then an article appeared about President Truman extending the draft, though he said he didn't expect to call anybody up. But on July 8 the *Times* printed a story about nine thousand guys in the county being eligible. That had to include me, too. And there was a lot of talk about the possibility of another world war. On July 12 a story said that over a hundred guys in their middle twenties had been given pre-induction physicals, which meant if the war lasted very long, they'd eventually get down to me. With each passing day the headlines got bigger and bigger, and the number of stories appearing on the front page about the war grew, until they filled it. And then one day I saw a photo of my friend Bill Miller on the front page, dressed in Marine Corps uniform. Bill had enlisted right after graduating with the class of forty-nine. Under the photo it said that he was now in Korea, serving with an engineer battalion. Ham, too, had begun to worry; he was closer than me to the age of the draftees.

When I got back to the flat, after I had signed with Maynard Morris, there was a letter waiting for me. It was from Mom, telling me that my draft notice had come, and I had to go home because I'd been scheduled for a pre-induction physical.

So here I am, in the army. I took basic training at Fort Knox, and then was sent to Germany, where I am now. My first post was an armored cavalry regiment, in Amberg, a tiny little village an hour's drive from Nürnberg. I was a tank driver. Our mission was to patrol the border of communist Czechoslovakia, because of the Cold War. We were told we were a frontier outpost. If the communists in Eastern Europe decided to invade Western Europe, we would be the first ones to receive a hit—and that it was our duty to hold off the whole friggin commie forces, until the NATO armies could set up a defense. At that time, the Korean War had reached a crisis. There was a lot of sabre-rattling in Eastern Europe, rumored to be a military diversion. The effect on us was one of constant alert. The call usually came in the middle of the night. We dressed hurriedly, scrambled into our tanks and other armored vehicles, and sat in them, motors idling, till dawn, when the all-clear sounded. I don't think any of us ever believed it was the real thing, but there was always the fear. Actually, what we feared most was the poor state of our armored vehicles, tanks included, half of which had engines that wouldn't start on any given day, and in the event of a real invasion we would have been sitting ducks. And there was a reconnaissance airplane, a little single-engine Piper-type that sometimes strayed over to the Czech side and got shot at, the pilot's ass saved by a plate of armor screwed to the bottom of his bucket seat. We feared his poor navigating would start a war. All of this led to days and nights of either nagging fear or mind-numbing boredom.

Soon I learned I could escape all that by volunteering to attend schools that no other G.I. in the company would go for, our first sergeant having been ordered to send "volunteers" to various schools. So I volunteered. Anything to get out of that place! I sat through Tank Turret Mechanic School in Vilseck, Motion Picture Projectionist School in

Bayreuth, and the Non-Commissioned Officer's Academy in Munich, all of which took me away from that "frontier outpost" most of the time. While I was at one of these schools, the Seventh Army Repertory Theater rode onto the post one day and performed a comedy. Lo and behold, one of its performers was a classmate at the Neighborhood Playhouse! Boy, was I glad to see him! I asked how he got this great duty. He told me he pretended to be a little crazy, so they put him in Special Services. He pulled a few strings and got me transferred. And now I'm stationed at Seventh Army Headquarters, in Stuttgart, and serve with the Seventh Army Repertory Theater. We travel around Europe and entertain G.I.s, but we have a lot of time on our hands, and that's how I came to write this story. Writing it chased away the boredom, during the long weeks when we weren't scheduled anywhere. Incidentally, Ham too was drafted, but was soon discharged because of "poor health." He has returned to the flat on Twelfth Street and has got a job writing dialogue for a soap opera—*The Secret Storm.*

And I guess this is as good a place in the story as any, to say that my Neighborhood Playhouse classmate Joanne Woodward has already become a big movie star, with her name splashed all over theater marquees, but I suppose you know that already.

It's been almost five years, since that first day of my second senior year, the day I felt so ashamed I waited till everyone passed by the house, so no one would see me slinking up the street to school. I consider myself a new person. I can even say my parents' troubles don't bother me so much any more. Which is to say Mom and Dad and I get along a little better. But even today, their marriage still hangs in limbo, and Mom still sees George. Dad has moved to Sandusky, Ohio. He sold his franchise in commercial refrigeration, and he has a new business: he sells new glass and aluminum store fronts to retail businesses in northwest Ohio.

In case you want to know about my plans for the future. It's May 1954, the Korean War is over, and my two-years of active duty will end next month. When I get back to the States, I plan to return to New York and pick up where I left off.

Before I stop, there's one more thing I have to tell you about.

I had just put the finishing touches to this story late one night. I fell asleep over it and had this dream. I was riding on the back of a yellow Cadillac convertible, top down, in a parade. I was the center of it. I had just finished a run on Broadway, playing the leading role in *Hamlet*, and Mayor Mahanavich had invited me—the celebrity actor—to a homecoming in Coaltown. The Cruhl High School Coal Digger Band was leading the way down Main Street. The curbs were lined with smiling faces, and arms waving warm greetings: Señorita Witherspoon waved the paper that held the Armistice Day speech; Miss Marlowe waved my King Lear beard; Old Gussie waved, her head wrapped in a turban made of boys room toilet paper; Gloria Vane shouted greetings in pig latin; and even Feralman—waving his torn lapels. The parade came to a halt in front of Old Peg Leg's house. She was standing on the porch holding the book of poems, its spine broken. She opened it and held it out to me. Suddenly a gust of wind came up and took away the pages, one by one, like birds in flight. I leaped out of the car, dropped to one knee in her front yard, and began to recite the poems in the book, having learned them all by heart. And then I woke up.

Tucker Amory's 2nd Senior Year

by Jack Smith

Shenango River Books, No. 4

Cover art and design
by Mike Reznor

Designed and set
in 12 point Times New Roman type
by Asparagus Studios
for Shenango River Press.
Sharon, Pennsylvania,
Summer, 1996.

Printed by C.F.E. Printing,
Grove City, Pennsylvania

Shenango River Books
Box 631
Sharon, PA 16146

About the Author

Jack Smith has taught high school English, led workshops for schools and colleges, and served as curriculum consultant in English for the Pennsylvania Department of Education. Today he is Lecturer in English at the Shenango Campus of The Pennsylvania State University in Sharon.

His poems and scholarly essays have appeared in literary magazines and academic journals.